MW01245518

# QUERENCIA SUMMER 2023

QUERENCIA

Querencia Press, LLC
Chicago Illinois

QUERENCIA PRESS

© Copyright 2023

**All Rights Reserved**

No reproduction, copy or transmission of this publication may be made
without written permission.
No paragraph of this publication may be reproduced, copied or
transmitted save with the written permission of the author.

Any person who commits any unauthorized act in relation to this
publication may be liable to criminal prosecution and civil claims for
damages.

ISBN

978 1 959118 64 0

www.querenciapress.com

First Published in 2023

**Querencia Press, LLC
Chicago IL**

Printed & Bound in the United States of America

# CONTENTS

# NON-FICTION ................................................................................. 163

# ABOUT THE CONTRIBUTORS ........................................................ 212

# POETRY

**My body is a graveyard – Cara** (she/her)

Rough and pitted like worn stone
all the things that refuse to heal
because recovery requires blood
and decay takes that first.

My eyes are sunken ships of things
reminding me that I am
more loss than water
more age than laughter
and the butterflies never seem to come to me anymore.

The vultures crow victory and these tendons sing back promises of
soon, soon, soon.
When my daughter died, I asked the moon to take me with her but
of course there is no lunar
forgiving and her cold light only amplifies the rattling in my chest
where my heart should be.
My lungs are mausoleums which entomb the air I held for you,
preserved for it was precious.
At least to one of us.

There is no door, but if you look closely at my nose you'll see it is
plastered with something like wax,
a stopper for this mind which disintegrates so easily but if you see
me dreaming and lost, let me be.
Let me live in the corridors of my head for there are so many roads
undiscovered there
and if you see something that glimmers like brilliance, just note that
I am rich in dead futures
and broken prophecies.

It's a gateway, not really me
but I think I enjoy the blurring between.
The grey forest is more familiar than her eyes ever were and I think I
heard my funeral song.
Now don't kid yourself, it's not a curated selection by those who
knew me well,
they're all still sporadically ringing my notification bell but the
destruction in smoke
tastes something like home.

I'm not convinced I was ever born of my mother, but rather the
asylum where the delirium drifts
with souls who were left too open, never fully closed by the skinlike
trapping
god was supposed to enclose.
I suppose,
that feels better.

I am but an unfinished letter, stray thought,
the tarnished top of an iron wrought fence which had purpose and
value once.
I muse that I must have had too but not in this life.
So if my shape ever blurs into inhuman lines, just know.

I was never meant to be here. I am trying, though.

**the five stages of grief are as follows: the cleave, the bleed, the hollow, the shattered and the forgotten – Cara** (she/her)

ONE: the cleave
It is the unrecovered black box in a devastating crash.
I have never found the words to accurately depict it
though I relive every detail.

TWO: the bleed
he'sdeadhe'sdeadhe'sdead
   phonetheambulance911isn'tright
this isn't right
   i can't feel my hands
         what if i crack a rib
               BREATHE
                my lungs are iron his- hands are blue
  and when did all colour flee from the room?
        when has a morning ever forgotten to dawn and there's
        nothing left to do—
              they turned left
they.      turned.      left.
i've never smiled so mirthlessly
        it doesn't matter now does it

THREE: the hollow
a collection of shower thoughts while the water beats all feeling
from my shoulders

a) if there's a god do you think I can trade my life?
b) i can understand the razor appeal but I don't know if I'm more
afraid that it won't hurt.  still.

c) it's not even a colour is it? not grey or black, it's that it no longer matters and the sunlight can stream through me, translucent.
d) i tell people that a little of me died when he did. not enough though.
e) are we sent depression so we can practise death? i remember a description in a book once and it chilled my blood, the theft of it all. i was so scared that would be me. it's not so scary though is it?
f) i'd love some orange juice. too bad the corner shop is multiple realities away.
g) the notifications are hollow reminders that out there...
snapchat has a new filter available. do you think it'll even out?
drown it out? douse me in colour
that I might burn all the faster

FOUR: the shattered

you know that script song that goes "and the sixth is when you admit, you may have fucked up a little."? Here's where you bury yourself in reflections of mistakes, futures faded and fickle fucking sparks of hope that end up rope to strangle you with.
have you ever swallowed after you've burned your throat? walked in the dead of winter alone? seen in painful clarity who you could have been before you throw up all over the floor?
the tantalising closeness of home then foreign
given but borrowed
interest choking avenues of escape
and so many different photos to cling to the possibility
you could still be alive
still be something else
something new
instead of lighter fluid blue
FIVE: the forgotten

it was his birthday...
whether you watched the clock in agony or forgot,

      there are no balloons for dead boys. no 21st.
          no living long enough that he might even be
                heard.

his death steals words from your lips
measured only in missed
lost longer than loved

some things you don't get back.
for that attack,
there is no defence.
no density of words which can fix you.

some things you can only lose.

**the fool – wren pflock** (they/them)

being with her was better
than i could have imagined
i was never without fear
insecure to the highest fault
but i'd set my body alight
to do it all again with her
i fool myself during the day
that i'm okay with this
that i don't miss everything
that i don't want to crawl into her bed
just to hear her breathing
i pretend anything else could fill me
the way her voice did
the way the adrenaline did
the way touching her did
thighs pressed together on a train
head sleeping on my shoulder
on the bus back from a party
that i begged her to come to
i try to find it in myself to be mad
i should be furious
but it only devastates me
how much her actions have hurt me
and how much i want her despite them
i feel tragic and irrational and dumb
because i know nothing lasts
i promised myself too young
that i would never be hurt by love
because i decided too young
that love is not real

age has only made a fool of me
as i've fallen in love with her
against all rational thought
i would do it better this time
risking the gut-wrenching pain
and the sucker punch ache
that i received from the second-hand news
i would do it all again
i've turned from a sensible child
to the fool dancing in the sun
setting over the apocalypse
burning up for a girl
who gave me whiplash

**FORGET BEING GOOD; CAN I JUST BE MYSELF? – April Renee**
(she/her)

mama spoke in terms of the ten commandments. daddy expressed himself through sloppy blows. the priest trained me to be an altar girl, to always be of service. taught me that helping is holy while caressing the small of my back. i don't know what holy is supposed to mean anymore. i am confused about morality. i was taught that to be good was to be god-fearing, but i've found that most people act irrationally when driven by fright. being raised as a woman in the church, i learned early that personal fulfillment comes from meeting other people's needs. i get off on graciously gutting myself for the kin, for the comrades, for the cause. i only play the part of an empowered woman. in reality, i am obsessed with self-sacrifice. i wish i could turn off the part of my brain that pines for perfection and simply exist in my own body. stroke my fair skin, soft and supple, and shush my desire to be a good host to anything but my own heart. i don't want to spend the rest of my life trying to be wholesome when all i really want to be is whole.

## STAGE FOUR SEX – April Renee (she/her)

your mouth greets me like a crack in the rocks in a tidal zone—
urgent and wet. milkworts grow freely down your backside and my
hands frolic in the sand for a moment. i know you like that. lean in. a
graze of your lip against my pink-tipped ear,      *how was your day?*
       who cares? who cares about anything but the small gap
between us, begging to be filled? my wanting you is similar to a kid
waiting for school to get out. i am running as soon as you ring the
bell. i am preoccupied with the span of your arms, long enough to
engulf me and spin me like a torpedo to the bedroom. i am being
torn limb from limb. my discarded outfits litter the mattress, but it's
no matter to us because we are here. spread out like an aggressive
cancer, taking each other quickly and quietly and not without pain.

## HEAT WAVE – April Renee (she/her)

my stuffy, poorly painted bedroom swelters and restless calves kick the sheets to the side like last year's trend. i can't sleep. the heat draws the tears from me like it soaks the last drops of water from the soil. pins me down with its oppressive thumb, manicured by the commanding hand of god. it beats me clean, blood rinsing my muddied mouth, bruises blooming around each retina: *you have such beautiful eyes*. the saccharine sentiment of summer sticks to my sweating lip, trying to deceive me into believing something so torrid could ever quench my thirst. summer love is a lie. it is only ever delirium delivered by those who have never melted under the tongue of september's sorrow. promoted by the lucky and the well-groomed, who have never had to lick their wounds beneath the leaf of autumn's anguish. i fell in love on the fourth of july once. had my back scratched under the stars. had my cheekbones stroked beneath a dark velvet curtain, which was just a stage for heartbreak but i didn't know that then. the thing about summer love is that it is more of an idea than a concrete action. it will turn people into poems and poems into long laments. it will spit into your mouth under the sheets and in your face the next day. suddenly, it will break like a high fever and none of it will seem real (because it wasn't.) the leaves will begin to abandon their branches and the tree in your backyard will start to bleed sap. you'll see a metaphor in this. the season's fingers will loosen on your woeful throat and you'll realize you've been choking on steam for months. you'll realize you never needed a summer love. you just needed the heat to let go.

## LITTLE I LOVE YOUS – **April Renee** (she/her)

your slow tongue along the curve of my earlobe
the way you brush my shoulders off after zipping up my dress
your tender hands mopping up my vomit in the middle of the night
how you stroke my wet, tear-streaked chin
your bum in a lawn chair so that i can stretch out on the whole
couch
the extra salt you throw on the corn just to satiate my midwestern
taste buds
your arm across my chest when you brake too fast
the heavy things i never have to lift
the light things you've given weight to
the way you say it:
*baby, come to bed.*
like i am what you've been looking forward to all day.
*baby, come to bed.*
like i am your best friend.
*baby, come to bed.*
like you couldn't get a wink of sleep
without me.

**OLD FASHIONED – April Renee** (she/her)

fastening his boxers to the line, pinching them gently with pruned fingers and unpainted nails, she hums to herself and fantasizes that the overgrown yard is her very own empty stage. in her head, she is a young Loretta, even though she knows she will never see lights like Nash. even though she knows she will never be brave like that. Loretta would leave his underwear in a wet ball and write a hit song about how he's a no good cheatin' turkey, but she just can't do something so brazen. she loves him in the way that no woman should, in the way that siphons the sanity from her tank and leaves her sputtering and spitting on side of the highway. meanwhile, he plays footsies with some raccoon-eyed distraction in a tavern painted with lead and lies. it's not that she doesn't care but that she is afraid of what it would be like not to love him. so she'll stay here and hang the underwear. hum. roll the dough for dumplings. and when he does come back, smelling of cheap cherry body spray, she will do what any kind-hearted woman does

say welcome home, love.
are you hungry?

**ROT GIRL SUMMER! – Mousai Kalliope** (she/her)

Let the ingenuous darling linger in a state of yearning.
It is rot girl summer and
**She. Shall. Rot.**
Sour honey drips from a corner in her mind,
*Desire.*
But, oh, she knows *nothing of all things.*
All things that make a girl into a woman.
The sharp blisters exploding red because of the heels, the smudged red lipstick adorned with tears, pink ribbons lost to men and their need to
Tear apart.
Let Ms. Darling enjoy the fantasy world in her daydream, her dreams and expectations will be dust in a few more years. The sun won't shine like it does now.
(*The sea will call for her sacrifice soon*)
And she'll learn how to be porcelain and cold, colder than the ignorance itself. With a soft voice pronouncing the word "yes" over and over again.
*Pulpy black plum juice is spilled into her lap, and she dips her hands in it, fucking feral. Drags it across her lips, the soft squishy pulp, eats it, looks in the mirror:*
—*What am I? Just to feel something.*
**Could you blame her?** *She will not live longer than 16.* That's when hope fades away and is replaced by a giant wall of concrete. Could you blame us? Women...for being
Insane?
Pulp is smeared on her face,
—*It's ok. I'm still in control.*

*Was she ever?*

**chatting on omegle with a conversation partner or a firewall –
tommy wyatt** (he/they)

Ω omegle talk to strangers!                    you're now chatting
                                               with a random
                                               stranger. say hi!

you both like *am i gay quizzes* and *Saint Maud* (2019).


**stranger:** those results are pure acetone to pour directly

**stranger:** onto your fuchsiascorched eyes,

**stranger:** the results always burn a little longer and you apply

**stranger:** the pain like polish because she peers into you, your

**stranger:** body firedissolved and warm with sick

**stranger:** and wanting, asking about your latest horse phase

**stranger:** by gesturing to your horse necklace that doubles

**stranger:** as a mood reader, the color always black; she asks

**stranger:** how you are, your screen blinking you to

**stranger:** dissociation, where you slip into the day you wished

**stranger:** for it, another girl bought it for you at the bookfair

**stranger:** singed by the smell of rotted flora, musty like your

**stranger:** youthstained period blood she fingered out of you

**stranger:** and you're popped out of choice for desire, she

**stranger:** bought you that necklace and *Black Beauty*

**stranger:** and forced you to touch yourself when you used

**stranger:** them and she'd touch herself and she leaned in to spit

**stranger:** on your horse necklace and rubbed it clean of

**stranger:** demons since possession is contagious even as she

**stranger:** sickens the promise of jesus, the horse in doomblack

**stranger:** plagued by her, she begged you to pray with the tease

**stranger:** of her tongue. maybe you were afraid and maybe you

**stranger:** were wet with wanting because soon you'd need

**stranger:** to melt yourself into a fuchsiaburned fleshpuddle

**stranger:** and it glitters in the sunlight or the eye of fire

**stranger:** like the feeling of a fresh cut on your virginwrists

**stranger:** and you'll be afraid that she'll swallow you clean

your conversation partner has disconnected.

start a new conversation. or <u>save this log</u> or <u>send us feedback</u>.

**how to cope (note: in an unhealthy way only) / how to identify who said "let's run out of consciousness for once" / how to become a ghost – tommy wyatt** (he/they)

*who am i when my consciousness is mangled by the teeth i had ripped out of me when i was 3 and i wasn't even granted the salve to sleep, to when i dream of anesthesia and throw melatonin gummies back as a hail mary, to when i am in your soft boiled hands and how you jaundice my body with touch and i am trying so hard to scrub it out in the shockheat of a hundred showers and it feels like i watched the house of wax too young again and i worry my skin will peel off in sticky starched patches especially when i ask if my body is allowed to be mine, to when i'm a teen again just waking up in the crisp hospital bed, the light not even really white but blearing and wet and haunted?*

**NOT A CYOA MEMORY, SORRY KID – tommy wyatt** (he/they)

**NARRATOR**

You have a story, TOMMY. You almost died once. You haven't eaten for days and woke in the lavatory, hazy with mist from the shower running, in heavyfluorescent whitebrightness. (Try to make it look like TOMMY is thinking about how he hopes he was any cast member from *Poltergeist* and, just, maybe would be cursed to die?)

(The lights go black for a moment, the projector flashes a starry sky. The night billow outs as the lights fade back on.)

Yes, in that quick moment, you're strapped in the car, your eyes follow the road until it slopes to a sunshine logo'd motel. (Try to make it look like TOMMY is thinking about his *last* vacation. Was it his *last* vacation?)

You swallowed *Heaven* by Bryan Adams down like a spoke. Your eyes went bright, like cartoon stars when the dude's about to pass out from laughing at a good joke you don't understand. (The curtain, pittering, is an expression of time.)

What happened right then, when you went away? Would you call it a case of the strange and bizarre sudden loss of time? Would you call it a turgid evil festering in your body and call it sickness, or a concern for an exorcism? Is there really a difference when the pain possesses you? Or would you call it what it really is: dissociative black out? You'll stay, TOMMY. You'll wake up in vague lighting from your littledeath simulator corroding a mess of your vision.

**happy valentines day? love, schadenfreude – tommy wyatt** (he/they)

holographic hearts on a valentine's card: *is it* 4th grade, when you tried to hide the hazy sun with your blanket even though there were scarier things to hide from,

*is it* much later when you're 14 and *socalled* unfeeling doctors are concerned about your pain more than anyone else whose only concern should be you and *if* you're in pain,

*is it* your monitor shattering the illusion to deadred pixels and you're in your midtwenties and you can't breathe and Peanut cries to find you while you tell your partner

how much it hurts and they make time to be with you through night that twists and churns in your throat and your AI chirping in its autotuned voice *this isn't normal*,

*is it* when you realize now that you hide so much fear and sick and pain from it all because you grew up believing it was fine your parents will always love schadenfreude

a lot more than you.

*it is* because it's never you.

**the future as an omen – tommy wyatt** (he/they)

see the cat hiding under the bed, pupils sharpening as this predator in the distance mimics her human's voice better than she can chirptrick her way to birds, the way the air wrinkles cries and dissolves them in rain? it's the same as the kid from *Skinamarink* glowering at the pupilpitched darkness under her mother's bed, with nothing but the abyss staring back and a voice cutting through the fugue with, "you know we love you very much," and how much do you blame yourself now for perceived survival, even as you puke it out, even as it possesses you?

sorry, possession is a too heavy charge? it's 2023, you know, *Yellowjackets* is doing it and, like, you're saying you don't have a negapersona that shovels dirt down your throat?, but you do have religious documentaries and *The Exorcist* flickering on a bubbledged screen from 2003, your dad saying he's channel surfing (with static between to prove), and things you dissociate through to survive. you know, the thing you said was "almost fainting" when your parents collectively asked *what was the matter with you, why weren't you listening?* you know that you were doommoding before you could ever form a solid identity? and the charge of possession means you can claim whatever until your voice breaks, everything that makes you strange intensifies like the potential pain from a sunharnessed magnifying glass, as your vision lapses time, as in rewind?

you can walk to Blockbuster, it's okay, it's 2003. you can return the tape now. you'd want to return the tape now, can you imagine the fees if you blink and it's suddenly 2023?

**A Glacier's Glide – Daniel Moreschi** (he/him)

An arctic glacier crawls across a frozen floor,
while waves of steely clouds abound, compound and pour
their snow onto its lucid bastions, forming streaks
that slowly fortify its crevasses and peaks.

It ventures onwards through a powdered valley where
it's ardently caressed by frets of errant air.
Cacophonies of eerie wheezes backed by wails,
attune with sudden swirls that circle on the trails

as frigid fragments rise again in unison;
revolve, converge, then flit in stintless fits that run
with unseen swoops. The structure still maintains a base,
outlasting hoary dawns whenever they retrace.

Its fronts and sides show signs of tumult-sculpted drapes
with countless layers turned to shattered shards. The scrapes,
meanwhile, reflect a brimming myriad of gleams,
like sun-brushed constellations seized by icy seams.

It navigates a steep meander and suspends
within an unforgiving depth of briny beds,
while treading rocky sinks that rend an inner quake.
A pillar wears expanding fractures. Ridges break

up into rains of milky dust. A sheet erodes
in rows of ruptured roars. An ailing bridge unloads
its decks as walls come crashing down. The remnants stay
to coat an ocean with a crystalline array.

**Flesh Amnesiac – Sadee Bee** (they/she)

Ridges of fingerprints, caress the silk of this skin. Eyes dine
on the saturated glow of its blush. The mauve hidden between
the brown, a divine delicacy. Not a banquet for the masses, no,
a dark dessert for the wanting.

*There is always someone wanting.*

Craving satiation. A ravenous need to consume all
that I have coveted. These lips, a tincture of Belladonna.
Disguised by the sweetest whispers of all you beg to hear.
Forget yourself in the intoxicating, bittersweet scent on my breath.

*This flesh is not for remembering.*

**Under the Stepping Stones – A. Bhardwaj** (she/her)

In the dew-strung early mountain mornings
before the first coffees burble and songbirds nestle deeper into
warm boughs
two cousins commence a search.

We upturn flowerpots, wave apologies at disgruntled slugs
who snort, remembering their own young.
We traipse through sodden grass, whispering good mornings
ignored by still-sleeping spiders.

Dirt speckles our knobby knees, veggie-patch worms
making room for child-size hands that turn up
nothing at all.

Down the street, a car horn honks
Two doors over, a dachshund barks as
the dance teacher's bhajans waft through the leaves.
Morning settles over the valley and
the explorers trudge home,
empty-handed.

You will not find snails in the morning's soft light,
nor the inbetween hour of night and dawn.
Snails do not linger like local foxes, leaving
the odd, lonely track in fresh mud; immortalized.
Snail trail magic lies in impermanence.
The first time I happened on a snail:
Midnight, crawling through sharp bushes scratching my cheeks,
calling for the neighbor's dog,

fog lay heavy on the earth, obscuring that small magic.
My palms broke the fall
on a weathered stepping stone.

Tucked safe in the moonlit shards,
a small spiral.
Within its shell, the depths of the world.

You cannot find snails by digging blindly in flower patches.
Snails live not on the leaves of morning glories, but in the dark in the
midst of some sweet nocturne.
Of the shadows they bloom, and in those negative spaces
the gnarled, snagging root balls of soaring oaks,
the undersides of moss-slicked wooden bridges,
the cool liminalities where time slows underneath stepping stones
in those dark spaces, where you seek not search, by happenstance
you stumble on a snail.

You look down at the coil
cradled in your hand,
an ancient tiny god who walked hundreds of millions of years before
you, in this moment, unearthed.

**notes on reproductive labor – Willow Page Delp** (they/them)

Reproductive labor is:

1. The work necessary to the reproduction of human life, such as having and raising children. / *(Why am I the one doing this? She's not my daughter.)* / It is often considered work that people should be happy to do. / *(I'm tired.)* / Vital for the maintenance of the labor force. / *('What are you talking about? You didn't do anything today. I was the one working. You don't get to be tired.')* / Often invisible / *(I took care of her, cleaned her messes, dried her tears, kissed her forehead, and told her how much I loved her.)* / Not understood within a formal system of work, wages, and production / *(Not understood.)*

### Motherwound – Sara Sabharwal (she/her)

I have existed only in the absence of true connection.
No invisible strings tie me to anything, as they have all been severed
as umbilical cords from mothers.
No womb has ever housed me, allowed me to grow, to flourish.
I have no home.
Walking aimlessly in this abyss.
This carefully curated collection of features, a chameleon, morphing
to fit the aesthetic of what is around me.
I seep slowly into wallpaper in rooms—camouflaging myself
Did you know you can make small talk with a ghost?
Screaming internally—
Love me,
Accept me,
See me.
But instead,
I see their strings flow from one to another.
I see mine, limp.
Dangling from a heart one beat away from hollow—
A soon to be black hole that will engulf my entirety.
But—
I have existed only in absence.

**Exodus – Sara Sabharwal** (she/her)

They say,
Hell is empty—
The demons linger here.
Where is your god,
Has he just disappeared?
Aren't captains meant to go down
With their ship?
I find it hard to forgive this abandonment,
This existence of hellfire and torment and
They say free will is a gift.
Bibles clung to as life rafts
Then hung as nooses around necks
Of those who sin differently than you.
Pay your dues,
Sit in pews,
Certainly this will save you.
Abandon the poor,
Turn a blind eye to abuse.
Your God or your humanity
Which will you choose?

**Flowers Without Petals – Dan Flore III** (he/him)

I almost feel like myself
sitting here with
a sugar high
under the wet diaper sky
going home to read the Bible
to live in a different world

and I used to be so thoughtful
now these words just point at me
to write them
as if they mattered
as if I did

dream of me sometime
in a pina colada sky
when things were better
can't you just almost see me smile?

## Me and the Mean Looking Lady – Dan Flore III (he/him)

I passed this lady on the street
she looked at me really meanly

I don't think she was mad at me though

I think it was just the strain
the putrid
no good strain

I know I've looked at people
meanly
but it was just all the bullshit
getting squeezed out my eyes like ooze

pray with me mean looking lady
our beautiful eyes
were meant for so much more

## Revisions – J.D. Gevry (they/them; fae/faer; he/him)

*CW: This poem employs a metaphorical allusion to non-consensual sexual experiences*

I knelt timidly astride his neck
hovering          in welcome invitation
—I can't do it—sun-naïve parts
on fullest display

they were taught
gynophobia—trans stigma—misogyny—
Fear. they held shame like a shield and
normalized neglect

my desires live in the clashing vibrations
of yearning and excitement
hesitation and fright, shivering
in their pulsing undulation

post-surgical protrusion—paid for with
blood and
crisp bills
left on dressers—ignored beside that

lush opening favored by men
like a prize: in my love
healing them
but       they sometimes

steal like bread
when they hunger
to hurriedly pull apart    in solitude
and consume as nourishment

his firm hands clasp resistant hips, my
half-moon seashells dragged ashore
that      crooked-smiled mouth
waiting and cocky

*sorry*—my coy confession—*I'm shy*

« *don't be shy* »

he said, honey-pace from under
eyebrows lounging heavy
with the seduction      only
mischief can bring

silently capturing me
with      tender command:
*bring yourself to me*—
*welcome me unto you*

he lifted his mouth, engulfing the asset I keep
locked away in my basement      like a secret
that same quiet, cool confidence
he always has   what an asshole

and my lips still curl      like a leaf
red ridges folding in on
summer's memory:
letting go in his play

my exposure      and embrace
pleasure caught
and displayed
in his beard

**I'm Not Ready Yet – J.D. Gevry** (they/them; fae/faer; he/him)

*CW: This poem is a graphic expression of a non-consensual sexual experience.*

I love him I want him he's sexy so sweet We've gone once already
we're back in the sheets *I'm not ready yet  I'm not ready* I said  *I'm
not ready yet* but he goes right ahead He repeats what I say that *I'm
not ready yet* I know that he heard me *I'm not ready yet* But he
plunges inside  and I don't understand  Cuz he heard what I said
he's not 'that kind of man'  I know that he heard me  *I'm not ready
yet*  He repeated my words I think just in jest Shock bolts through
my body unsure what to do Cuz I want him just not now  need
foreplay need lube  And it's too late he's in me *I'm not ready yet*
And I know that he heard  and I meant what I said  But I love him
and want him soon it'll feel good Just didn't start off the way that it
should Said *I'm not ready yet* looking square in his face Said ok
that's ok  to reclaim my space  His eyes flashed a look I think that he
knew  I'd said *I'm not ready* my betrayal showed through I think that
he saw at least lack of laughter

so I didn't say more

———————————————

and we didn't talk after.

**The Day Everything Changed – J.D. Gevry** (they/them;
fae/faer; he/him)

West Coast departure, my lover
awaiting partner reunion
his permanent move
        Permanent.

"I'm so excited for you!"
even as veiled grief wept out
in rare
        unexpected red
flowing ruby-deep
from where he first entered

but I guess that's what love looks like
                              sometimes

**November 20th: This / Next / Last / Every – J.D. Gevry** (they/them; fae/faer; he/him)

 *—Dedicated to Fern Feather: a beautiful soul; stolen away. May she rest in peace and power.*

  *CW: This poem contains references to anti-LGBTQ+ bias and violence, including a graphic depiction of fatal anti-trans violence, as well as a reference to self-injury.*

I wonder what she felt as he scraped that knife through her ribs
 over and over, called it 'panic'
her Feather brown hair thick and wild, soft and flowing
as she was. One month of trans sisterhood—just out—and she's
already on that list of
Our dead; names uttered in wobbled monotone as expired prayers
lifted up
to the gray chapel of November sky, {stretching endless} as We
mourn those like Us
 We named it Day of Remembrance, but
  We remember.
Grief stacked like Our bodies they misgender
 even in death >> Another Sister's funeral, her family
speaking a name as  dead as she, laying there; so still, voiceless
  We do not speak of (god).
*Did you hear about her?*  I board up my windows and
wonder if he looked into her buggy brown eyes, their
Fern-glow ridges
 before he dumped her red pulp
 on the side of that country road I call Home
After the ¦Pulse¦ing mass of kills, the Red Cross collected blood
from the broken-hearted. Queers in a line, even knowing
 /they've banned Us\ from
saving our own; Our rejection certain since that epidemic—
Gay Cancer, they called it— We are
 still
surviving. So We sit this day ~unsettled as Our candlelight~
in community centers, coffee shops, the few churches that welcome

People Like Us; spaces made sacred by the magick We hold :: Once
chosen Shamans, now We hide
        arms
more scar than skin;  hearts
more pain than pump.  We do not speak of (god).  We
chant our chants and We sing our songs. We tenderly hang
photos of the stolen Us in front  with      carefully folded knock-off
Scotch tape, mostly femme Black and Latina faces          their
joyful lips painted red with
        ::Real Names::
underneath      We do not speak of (god).        this, Day to be
reminded; They are there, reminded
        We're still here, but
We remember—We don't need one annual day
for «wokeness-signaling» like them; digital posts
as quickly shared
as abandoned ¦ like my Siblings ¦        No,
We need just one day
        to forget

**Low Pile Fragments – J.D. Gevry** (they/them; fae/faer; he/him)

*CW: This poem contains anti-trans bias, kolpophobic speech, and graphic recollection of a non-consensual sexual experience.*

The words are plucking right there at my teeth
crowded inside and      standing nervously like
nape hairs that have known      Fear     before
Sitting in crossed-leg confession to my
best blanket friend:

a gay late night after-party : memory fractures

drunken, naked hot tub departure when they find out; start in
*not a real man : pussies are gross : we can't sit in this*
         *dirty water*

i see my hands on the carpet—low pile, beige carpet—
see them tensed, weight bearing
raw knee abrasions; scarred for months. gonorrhea from
...where?

i see my hands on the carpet

Someone is kneeling behind me
someone enters the room, sees

Leaves.

resisting force. Someone's hips pounding as cocained hearts;
i'm there i'm    not there      i
see my hands on the carpet : bang bang bang bang
ecstasy and booze? drugged?    immobile.      i feel nothing. Just

my hands
low pile carpet

: In silence        he bends at the waist
burrowing his bald head in my lap; a monk in wordless prayer.
I was the boy        burying his feelings
arm's-length underground, so our sorrow would not have
a chance to grow

I gathered his heaviest pieces in my arms, those
dampened elder tulips   split open
with the dwindling rains of spring
And we danced to shift weight

We fell into each other, there in the day-lit room
holding my hand through full-body pleasurequakes
crafting a juxtaposition: Then  and Now
wide as my weary, wintered sea
—

He knew
—

but said not a word, just kissed me in his arms
and loved away what hurt
just loved it all away

*Previously published under another name in *"Flush Left"* 2/2/23

## Quarantine, baby. – KRISTINE ESSER SLENTZ (she/her)

cakes for cats
meow remixes
trap measure
dog breeds back
meaning of carnation
flowers in the attic
exhaust fanned
napkin holder
toothpaste squeezer
juice cleanse
to heal prayer
candle lit
blue chip
and dale earnhardt jr
cheesecake factory
reset apple
online store hours
too minutes in a year
of the rake snake
game night
stand mixer
for vodka sauce
pizza dough
donuts delivery
food bazaar
magazine covers
letter of resignation
sample size
chart of accounts
receivable turnover ratio
test internet speed
of sound synonym
for authentic watches
brands of tequila
sunrise time
in new York
unemployment extension
cuts of cord blood
pressure cookers
pot roast
potatoes on the grill
say, *shut the fuck up*.

**blunder**
**of the box**
**instructions –**
**KRISTINE**
**ESSER**
**SLENTZ**
(she/her)

that feeling
Your face
feels after
crying in
Your sleep
lasts

boxed brownies
with extra
cinnamon and
cayenne pepper
and chocolate
chips bake
without sodium
but anger

how many
ways can I
say stop
speaking
because I
miss You

**Tabled – KRISTINE ESSER SLENTZ** (she/her)

finally spray paint project coffee table legs
press into area rug to wood floor
all the time—gravity
the way it is
did You write it
or was it logged
deep among brain folds
how do we love warmly
warm under wet supports
like bright duvet covers and digital
erasure makes homemade tequila cocktails

**please don't feed the bears – c. michael kinsella** (he/him)

I dream of simple things
Like filleting my government alive as they scream out "please don't feed the bears"
Then building homes from their bones to house the Hard to Home, as the entire god damn Parliament moans "please don't feed the bears."

You would think building bridges, paving roads, and burrowing tunnels would prove more difficult than getting a family out of the miserable rains that fall almost daily in the Fall.
Yet we don't call bridges The Hard to Build,
we don't call roads The Hard to Pave,
we don't call tunnels The Hard to Burrow.

We call them bridges.
We call them roads.
We call them tunnels.

Caged by sadistic societal standards, these animals (yes, we've fully dehumanized them) are a nuisance on the prestigious image our town counsel shows the world. These vermin have no worth, they're worthless. They hurt us, they are the burden nature birthed us.

Their flaws haunt us.
Their needs cost us.

The Hard to Value.
The Hard to Love.
The Hard to Acknowledge.

Still, we don't call tunnels Hard to Burrow, and please, do not feed the bears.

**Co-ICU, 2020 – Rachael Collins** (she/her)

You laughed about how anal sphincters relax at death,
The Great Equalizer,
And now I struggle to roll a sodden Chux pad from under your body.
Playing the music you said was your favorite
to drown out my chorus of
I'm sorry I'm sorry I'm sorry.

I'm sorry
For forgetting why you named your dog Johnny Depp
but remembering how I
zippered you into two body bags,
each Scarlet Lettered with a Sharpie's "C."
For when you cried for your mother and God but neither came,
as your panicked eyes recognized fear
in the mirror of my own.

In that moment my soul evaporated,
particles of cowardice suspended
like dust in the negative pressure room.
Afterwards sitting in the car with bloodshot and eternally dry eyes
while even angels weep.
And where is this God, for no one was there
when the watercolor bruises leaked around the ventilator tube in
your mouth
and I spilled Propofol on my shoes.

There are so many beds full of you,
and I'm just a moth pinned to the wall by the blue of my scrubs
while God still isn't answering our calls. So instead
Fairy Godmother, grant me forgiveness

for waiting to call security, not because I knew
the morgue and hallways were already pots boiling over with
bodies,
But because I didn't want to be left alone.

**Heart Plug – Rachael Collins** (she/her)

What a briar patch we find ourselves lost in.
My fingers are calloused from the lancets
Of countless, practice blood glucose checks.
Aurora pricking quivering finger
Over and over, to confirm the spindle still works.
A single drop of blood bestowed upon Accu-check strip
Protruding from Glucometer like clasped hands in prayer.

Diabetes is my second mother.
She slept between us every night
In a shared bed, after dad left.
and there was no one to guard against hypoglycemia
Always a few units of insulin or miles on the treadmill away.
Am I allowed to consider myself diabetic
While still owning a fully functional pancreas?

I had homework left undone but both hands full,
An orange in the left
And syringe full of water pantomiming as glucagon in my right.
Sword and shield against another visit from the paramedics.
Called in frenzied panic, shame climbing the back of my throat
The weekly presence of red and white strobe lights in our
apartment's driveway
A testament to my failure to keep her safe.

When mom's blood sugar is low
My hand encircles wrists that feel hollow like baby bird bones
And her skin has the clammy sheen of pig cadavers in a lab.
She's light enough to levitate, or you could carry her in your palm
from the counter she leans against, panting.

A sweetness to her breath and sweat, that of a soul saying goodbye.
Her body a dried out husk already, life evaporating with each
minute.

She screams and fights the EMT's,
their open hands and offerings of juice.
Shakes, whether with terror or incoming seizures, no one knows.
She'll later recount feeling like Alice slipping down a black hole,
that "the paramedics were coming to take my daughters away."
Not yet, mother.
Not yet, but soon.

Standing beside her hunched form wondering
When I'd grown so much taller
Or if she had shrunk
Sapped of inches the way so many lows leached her brain
Of people's names and normal cadence of speech.
Or perhaps I had always been the parent, the bigger one?

*"Heart plug,"* a goodbye mantra before school and at every friend's
house.
Reference to our connection, impossible to sever.
I needed no reminders,
Felt its invisible weight each time I rolled over in bed, a tug.
Calling hourly with "Is your blood sugar okay?"
"Please don't kill yourself," and
"I love you."

All powerful and yet powerless, an iron grip on air
with my words and glucagon rehearsals.
*Heart plug,*
Was it reassurance for me or for you?

And when the men did come
Were you upset by me being taken away
Or that I didn't turn around and look back.

**First Love – Rachael Collins** (she/her)

Probably never tasting sweet
But certainly fallen into at first sight, fast and hard.
Within weeks I peer through barred windows
At tiny ants milling two stories below, free.
"I don't know why I'm here."
Confused by the fish flip flopping where my heart used to be
Noodle of IV fluids slithering from my inner elbow,
Another pumping calories through my nose.
*When was the last time I ate a noodle?*
"My dog weighs more than you," the frizzy haired therapist remarks,
Unleashing twenty years of vicious competition
With every passing greyhound.

Two decades have passed and
I don't want to love you
But how do you disavow the only one who's always stayed?
The thudding of my messenger bag left a bruise on my inner calf
Yet for years I never adjusted its strap,
The dull ache, a homecoming.
I linger in the shower, savor its steam and hope to emerge reborn
Clean and wrinkled pink, a fluffy chick
Baptized of the desire for winged scapula.

"It's your one true love."
He spat the words like bloody teeth onto the ground between us
before walking out the door
Maybe for good this time, and yet, I feel nothing.
Except panic about dinner tonight, the whir of
*Toomuchyou'redisgustinggluttonouspigfixitgogogo*

Even now? At a time like this?
The rudest houseguest, entering without invitation and refusing to
leave.
But did I ever truly ask her to?

An empty plate such a small price to pay
for the absence of screaming.
You ask what my meal would be on death row,
Last supper before entering the most deafening silence.
My words, a prayer.
"Nothing."

**Jew-ish – Rachael Collins** (she/her)

"People like you are good with money"
*People like you.*

I keep my Jewishness with
the Star of David necklace grandma gave me
when I was five,
hidden in a drawer for when it will be safe to wear.
Removed from velveteen box from time to time
and examined at arm's length, twinkling
as my ancestors watch in disappointment.

There's Leah, my mother's namesake, who died
a jangling marionette of bones in the concentration camps.
Beside her, a great uncle with milky eyes,
Slashed by Cossack saber.
Their yellow felt patches sewn on with trembling hands
as I place my own star back in a drawer.
Is what makes me Jewish, this shame as I stand before them?

Parsley dipped in saltwater and charoset,
foods from an ancient home I've never known
left me praying to toilet bowls with a still undernourished soul.
As boys with shaved heads scream at the mall and I hide in plain
sight,
grateful for a "classical face"
while my sister prays to her patron saint, Barbra Streisand,
Guardian against nose jobs.

My Jewishness is Christmases tasting of wooden chopsticks,
lo mein and rice doused in sweet & sour sauce.

Aimless drifting past vacant shops
while envying children under twinkling trees.
Sunday school tastes of old grape juice and stale challah,
diaries written in half-learned Hebrew as code
and a forever memorized "Prince of Egypt" CD.

It's uneasy fantasies about great moments in history.
Fear I would not have risen to the occasion,
opportunities presented by the universe to be a hero.
Instead soft, human, surrendering honor and soul
for more time spent alive, cursing my cowardice
before death with the taste of shame heavy
like ashes on my tongue.

These tattooed arms exile me from Jewish graveyards
Wandering the desert of longing, undeserving of my God.

**The Feast of Us – Rachael Collins** (she/her)

Two sisters, paddling through a brothy riptide.
Climbing kitchen counters, outstretched fingers yearning
for cans of whole tomatoes or Campbell's or Spaghettios eaten cold,
always ever so slightly out of reach.
Greedy consumption of Food Network with insatiable eyes.

You wondered once if what we shared was love,
or simply memories no one else could understand.
Two soldiers standing on a hill,
looking down upon the remnants of a scorched battlefield.
I want to bathe you in a bowl of soup

until that golden brown crust of pain softens into the mush we once
were.
A man on the news said infants drown in bathtubs
so I showed you how to blow bubbles underwater.
Taught you to read with alphabet pasta letters,
scooped up in *"Here come the airplane!"* spoons

And gulped down into a warm belly
to grow hands that mix dough for challah and encircle steering wheels
as you leave and come back, leave and come back,
like the over-under of hair in twin braids parted down the middle
or dough longing for the brush of an egg.

Two girl-loaves, two stretched and braided and ovened,
heated like a promise.
Safe, sisters filled and filling with warm bread breath.
How simple it is to rest and become what you are
what you were kneaded to be.

## WHAT'S LEFT OF ROGER IS IN A ZIPLOCK BAG – Kelly Dillahunt
(she/her)

one that looks like it's been in grandma's cutlery drawer,
washed out and reused a couple of times

and now it's the last place a life's
being held together.

Some of Roger was shipped to Denver. Some flew
to Houston. Some is in a cemetery ten miles from
here, piled over his brother.

I plunge my hands into the plastic sack without
considering it, just another thing that
needs doing.

The ashes are coarser than firepit dust. I spread
Roger over the unopened peonies, the crooked trees, the place
where we burn things, the path with yellow weeds that
leads to the woods.

I spill Roger down my left side and into one
worn leather boot.

It's damp outside. Is that where
the raccoons keep getting into the attic? my brother

wonders, looking around the uneven yard that
was Roger's, that was Howard's, that's now our mother's,
the yard that's gone to shit complete with heaps of old
furniture and broken trailers and tangles of poison ivy.

It isn't windy and the ashes don't do what
they do in the movies, they just lay there, offwhite, almost
yellow, on the wet green grass.

The bag is empty and I want to throw it away. My brother says
It's only a bag.

I wipe my hands on my jeans and Roger
is there, now, too.

**I HAVE A TATTOO ON MY ARM THAT READS TRAILER TRASH** – Kelly
**Dillahunt** (she/her)

and I say y'all and soda, sitting next to grandpa whittling shapes
out of ivory soap

Knuckleheads, he called us, playing croquet in
the backyard. None of us know the rules or where
the mallets came from in the first place, sun gleaming off so many
red heads and necks, and that weed plant behind the shed growing
taller than the tin roof. The peach trees next to it never would
produce good fruit and besides, snakes live in the unruly gardens
beneath 'em

Bees buzz through the honeysuckle and rosasharons while
that rooster chases dad down again, me and the cousins
safe from its pecking, dirty feet pulled up on the porch swing,
and there's dump cake in the oven, out of a box and out of a can and
made with margarine and you can smell it all the way to the
above ground pool and red stained deck between the
crooked trees. Up early on Saturdays rooting out every
barn sale in the county, all of us crammed in with
three windows rolled down, ain't one of us ever had a car with
air-conditioning or four functioning windows

The pot plant and croquet set and ugly green peaches
are all gone now, half the family dead along with 'em, and
we google the difference between hemlock and
queen anne's lace, whatever-it-is growing thick through
the cracked hull of the overturned canoe next to the garage
full of raccoons.

## JET LAG – Kelly Dillahunt (she/her)

Trying to wend my way through
this feeble humid spring, cloudlit and tepid,
the sweet midwestern songbirds, that seven
hundred dollars' debt, my quiet
museum of a house, waking up at one am,
my body still in another time zone, worry over
insurance bills and tax returns and the next job,
the next job, always the next job.

I shut my eyes. Honey scented air and
a close sun, hot even at 70 degrees & cloaked in
spring wind. I wouldn't know to call this heat spring if
it weren't for the riot of flowers shouting from the hillsides.
Get out of bed tired and climb mountains, anyway,
rocky caldera beaches and slick marble
paving stones, shoes worn smooth
at the soles. Gritty black coffee. The raucous song of
parrots in sycamore, what is this place? It's not quiet anywhere,
save those dimlit churches halfway up the ridges; I've never heard
a hush that thick. There were tortoises fucking on
blue tile mosaics older than God.

Did I taste the salt of your skin, I swear I remember it

**Looking for god in a storm – Lesley Rogers Hobbs** (she/her)

I hike through woods until I arrive
at a clearing.
I speak to the evergreens
and question spiders dangling
from diaphanous webs. Breath bristles

the afternoon falters; I lean into
the snarled surface of the wind
and turn for home. Crows keen
as they abandon a lone oak; my eyes
trail the swirling black ribbon.

I will search for god tomorrow
in boots made for hunting
and gloves made of hope.

**A Visit to Craters of the Moon National Park – Lesley Rogers Hobbs**
(she/her)

Clouds swirl
and surround me
black lava and white snow-splatter
disappear into the drizzle.
The fog breathes—gray ghost
droplets coat my face and hair,
my hands press through mist;
I touch nothing but memories.

When I was fourteen, I spent
a glorious summer in Donegal,
the smell of turf damp and strong.
Black bogs and white capped
waves, dove-gray smoke
rising from chimneys.
I don't remember the sun shining
only endless silver sky.

They are not the same,
these lava beds
and the Donegal bogs
but I am incapable of
separating them.
The brume tendrils and twists,
tangles the truth
and I am home.

## Migration – Kushal Poddar (he/him)

The bird's whirring migrates here.
We have our reasons to move here,
never the right one.

We have lost our luggage. The bird
loses its first two attempted nests.
The weather hangs in tight, holding
a single vane, and the cock spins amock.

I look for the bird and when
some feathers float on the rill
I shiver, stay up until the noise
represents its presence.

**Pi Shapes An Irrational Number – Kushal Poddar** (he/him)

The clouds do a Buñuel.
Now the night bleeds into blindness;
now it sees more than it may

tolerate on the day it will recall
cast away underpants, sweating
held fresh in a perfume-bottle,
scent of a shattered vial gone stale
on a hoary carpet.

Splashed in that momentary bleeding
we stand midst the jettisoned picnic,
the cabin for lovemaking behind us,
your figure inks the smoke sign
rising from a deceased bonfire.

Sky, will your memory keep us safe?

**Fragmented Beauty – Meghan King** (she/her)

Falling in love with saccharine
Disillusion, confusion
Broke not broken
Shards of hope trust
Splintered desire, lust
Fragmented beauty
As a mosaic
Kaleidoscope spiraling
New foundation
Piece by piece
Built on strength and courage
Piece by piece anew

**Leaving Love in Brooklyn – Meghan King** (she/her)

Cold spring rains on the boardwalk as waves crash on the shore.
Midday sun breaks the cloud
A beacon, a hope

Allure faded

Coney Island melody from the rides

No longer our soundtrack

Pavement no longer sparkles

Rather just another street outside Nathan's
I put you on a pedestal, unconditional
You held all the ideals I had longed for
Honor, traditionalist, hard working
Semper Fi bred
On paper, my fairytale was one for the books.
In reality, I fell down the rabbit hole
Tripped into love


What can I say? Rose colored glasses
Sea mist clings to my jacket as I reminisce
Edison lights a reminder
Bedroom fairy lights haloed glow
Moments I had hoped for, thinking it'd never be
Head on your chest, falling asleep to your gentle snores
Knowing you were content peaceful
I thought waking up to you had been a dream.
Laughing on my couch, getting lit watching Jurassic Park
Creating weekend magic
But as it's said, *All magic comes with a price.*
Emotionally unavailable, both of us battling storms

I stop into a cafe, alone

Just down the block from The Bookmark Shoppe

Sitting at a table, condensation glistens on my ice coffee

No longer reminded of a chilled beer held to your lips

Not envisioning "what might have been"

Rather, embracing solitude

Sun streams through the window

As I sit at a table, droplets puddling around my cup

Opening a notebook, taking out a pen

Inspiration through healing

Watching traffic pass by

I smile to myself

Finding peace, not by your side

Peace in the courage it took to walk away

**Eighteen Months Old – Jasmine Luck** (she/her)

The topography of creases
On your tiny palm
Map out your heritage.
In Summer, your skin glows
A dusky olive, that's your Ahma,
Ocean-crosser.
Your curious eyes
Are bright blue; that's your Papa,
Himself a navigator
Of the world's underground riches;
Rocks, gems, soil.
Your shiny hair, carob dark,
That's mine, and your crescent
Lashes, to my envy, your father's.
These are the bedrocks
We have laid for you.
But my sweet baby, with every step,
Fingerprint, word,
You plot your own course.
Chart new territory,
Little mapmaker mine.

**Mixed Race – Jasmine Luck** (she/her)

The tectonic plates of my identity
Are shifting constantly.
With one foot in one culture
And one in another, the steadiness
Of my stance depends
On fault lines;
If the ground beneath moves too much,
How do I decide where I land
My feet?
Where do I fit within the landscape
Of faces, when I am two
Places, overlapping?
A patchwork childhood—jammy dodgers
Butting up against bee hoon, dried pork floss
And corned beef—provides stepping
Stones, anchors to both the worlds I move within.
And yet; I don't belong
fully here nor there.
A fact apparent in the frequent
Refrain of: where are you from?
More often than not, the answer
Is unsatisfactory, leading
To: where are you really from?
I can parse it. I know the real meaning:
"You look foreign.
Explain."

**Teeth – Kara Q. Rea** (she/her)

I chose your name.
The sharp edge of it cuts against my tongue
I can taste the blood

And I like it.
For a small thing,
It has bite.

Nature delivered you feral.
Furred and wild, serrated claws terminating
Into pointed vampire tips

They wrapped you in a blanket.
Soft and out of breath
You couldn't even cry.
They handled you as if at any moment
You would break.

But I knew
Beneath the pink newness
Underneath the skin
The tender gumline

You had teeth.

**In the Bones – Kara Q. Rea** (she/her)

117
Is what I write down next to my name.
The sheet slips and I see
The row of numbers for Jessica, Annabelle,
Blythe
The director's eyes appraise me in sections
calculating the sum of the parts
Are you sure? he asks. I nod.
The scale disagrees.

118.6
In this world, we stay inside the lines.
We've all heard the stories
of girls who did more than necessary
dipped far below the threshold
who weighed in with rolls of quarters
hidden inside their french twists
Grew their hair out heavy to their waists.
I told myself,
I should have shaved this morning
My head, my eyebrows. Every sodden lash.

117
Is when they sit me down with Oxchoa
so she can teach me how she fixed herself.
*It's all about the self controls, dear.*
She rolls the rs, rolls the pencil in her purple, bloodless fingers
Writes down 'boyled chickin, 4 ounce'
Her eyes gleam like wet gems in her cut-glass face
Every one of her bones casts a shadow underneath it

Later my partner looks at the paper on my fridge and laughs
*'Boiled chicken' my ass*, he snorts
*More like cock and coke.*

116
Is when I am
(presentable)
allowed onstage again.

113
Is when I stop in the middle of a show
and stand there frozen
glassy-eyed,
sweating in the hot white.
I've suddenly forgotten everything I know
About everything
Anything

112
*You can't keep doing this*, the director says in front of everyone
during notes.
*Yes*, I say. *I know.*
*Take some vitamins or something,* he advises. *Take a nap. You're a
fucking mess on wheels,*
*do you know that?*

109
Is when I can finally feel it.
Ethereal. Invisible.
A half-there will-o-the-wisp
hovering breathless over the abyss
Up at ten for rehearsals

Bed at six thirty.
Count the bones you can see
Feel for the ones you can't.
This is living.
This is staying alive.

103
Is when my partner holds my limp wrist in his hand
and clicks his tongue against the backs of his straight white teeth.
*Look at this! So tiny, like a baby bird!*
*And all this time I thought the problem was in the bones.*
*Honey,*
*Your bones are fine. Your issue is simple:*
*You're*
*all*
*Meat.*

100
is a nice round number
that I never end up reaching
Even though
my bones are fine,
so fine,
and the cage of my chest
has been scraped
hollow

**When I Think of Being Good – Kara Q. Rea** (she/her)

I imagine myself draped in indigo
Reciting from the apocrypha with
hands folded in my lap
(which I have never done) and
Definitely not
howling at my wildlings with the
Windows
Open (which I have done every day this
summer)
So wide the neighbors can hear the crimson
in my complexion, a vile, leprous fevering that came
from taking, taking, taking all that I could take
and then giving the rest away
And going to sleep
And waking up
and finding yet again that I am not good
Not even a little bit
and instead of folded hands
I pray with claws out
Greedy to snag onto a thread
from the hem of the garment
that can staunch this
Heavy bleed
this unholy run of
scarlet
Oh, Mother Mary,
I think you have a spot
On your reputation
but it's nothing a few millennia
and a little dab of soda water
can't fix

**Pickaxe – Liz Bajjalieh** (she/they/he)

The tiles of the bathroom floor
Felt like granite, I saw a pickaxe

Dragging parallel to the tracks,
Wandering alone besides the Amtrak train

Freedom finds itself most alive the moment
Before I fall asleep, the spasms,

The screams that tell my body
That I'm allowed to be here

And on the floor, I twist things up
I'm twenty one and a fool and a liberator again

And everything's fine, everything
Is as ripe as a fresh pear

## Second Class Scents – Jen Schneider (she/her)

When I was thirteen, a great aunt whom I never met gifted me a
gold elephant stuffed with lilac-scented cream. No chains or strings
attached. The elephant was beautiful in all ways I was not. Emerald
green eyes. Chiseled cheekbones. Exotic ears. Well-proportioned
limbs, lobes, and tusks. Adorned in rose. A balanced posterior. *More
or less.* The elephant's hollowed center had been repurposed and
transformed into a home for solid perfume. I found the concept
intriguing.

My own stomach was a gurgling abyss of teen angst. A butterfly
garden nested amongst basic intestines. Was it possible to curate
then store scents (and sense) in concentrated form? My thirteen-
year-old self was determined to know more. I slid the ornate object
onto heavy duty string (a tie-dye woven of purple, pink, and green)
and tied a knot around my neck. Each morning, I'd follow a similar
routine—cut twelve inches of cotton yarn then tuck my neck and
turn. The exotic elephant with the golden trunk quickly became an
essential component of my daily outfit. Both preparation for and
protection from boys belting ballads (off key) and girls playing
mean. Chastising and gossip regulars, along with mashed potatoes
and name-your-own flavors on the cafeteria tray. School halls (of all
grades) were rarely temperate. Too many trunks inappropriately
locked. Hormones on highways. Yield signs regularly denied. I'd
navigate packed herds of limbs and denim, often feeling more like a
cat amidst foul-smelling lions. We hadn't yet studied elephants. Also
hadn't been introduced to alternative forms of deodorant. I was
intrigued.

I turned to treaties and treatises. Encyclopedias and
advertisements. As I'd (t)read, I'd realize that, unlike the elephant,
most extended trunks could not be trusted. Like its namesake, the
mammal's perfume was neither becoming nor discreet. I didn't
care. I appreciated the extended space it provided when around my
neck. My orbit was suddenly wider. *More or less.* Only now do I
realize I had been misguided. The elephant never cared for the

butterfly. Just as my great aunt likely never cared for me. Like the elephant who never forgets, she was unloading and simultaneously ensuring her own memory. There's far too many ants working like bees. Far too many elephants climbing trees. Nobody asked for permission. Nobody contemplated weight. It's all a conspiracy. Like the women at the malls who'd give away free samples all while pining for a meager commission.

The elephant may have more scent receptors than any other mammal, they also fight back. Take mating season, as one example. The African elephant's 60% increase in testosterone production comes with its own unpleasant odor. Apparently, the female elephant finds rancid secretions intriguing. Scents and sense are confusing. *More or less.* Google confirms that solid perfume has been around for generations—it's a more economical choice. And that elephants are well-equipped with high-powered scents. Their sense of smell extends far beyond basic recognition to include quantity differentiation. Apparently, the elephant can distinguish between collections of small sunflower seeds, based on quantity, in ways that a human eye could never match. *More or less.*

Nevertheless, despite the power of the sense of smell, olfaction remains an understudied topic. While I've accepted that smell is often a second-class sense, olfaction and recollection formed, for me, many core high school memories. Pooled urine. Burnt butter. Fried Bunsen burners. Overused sweat socks. Underused deodorant sticks. Stuck in a routine (and at the back of the bus). Even the principal's office smelled of musk. He'd pass out cards to detention in the same dimensions as the sample strips distributed by perfume counters at the local mall. The same cards with peel-away scents that I'd collect most Saturdays, then sort and file as I prepped. For what, I think now—a coming extinction? The elephant in all rooms an invisible weight. Politics as masked as perfume. As I reflect on more and less, I wait—for truths, elephant style (and fresher scents). *More or less.*

14 (plus) reasons to smell (more than roses, oranges, and peppermint)

1. Sense and scents are homonyms.
2. Scent is not only the oldest sense, but also often the last sense to degrade.
3. The human nose can detect over a trillion different aromas.
4. Research confirms that women have a stronger sense of smell (and ___ ) than          men.
5. Observations and aromas often tango. Fear and distrust regularly present in sweat-infused aromas.
6. Scents are universal communicators. Soil holds scents like a lover.
7. Odor is nothing more than a chemical reaction.
8. Scents have seasons. Reason is just as often washed away as it is revealed with the rain.
9. Scents reveal decoys. Pores absorb more than potency.
10. Babies are born with a stronger sense of smell than any other sense.
11. The sense of smell is the singular cranial nerve capable of regenerating.
12. All humans have distinct odors. Idols also use deodorant.
13. Kings and Queens inhale florals just as often as favors.
14. All beginnings have ends. All ends have questions. Scents (and sense) are often first responders.

**Today (in February) – Jen Schneider** (she/her)

The sun rose early today—a minute earlier than yesterday and two minutes earlier than the day before. Time is funny that way. Solitary minutes stack like buckwheat flapjacks and Goodwill denim until, out of the ocean blue, a life—sometimes more, sometimes less, than a lifetime—concludes. Palms cupped. Cupboard bare. The EKG runs a flatline. The nurse nods, "It's time." Time mostly passes without notice, like today, until today. Just another ordinary February day. Then, it's gone. Eyes closed. Winds whisper. I yawn.

I remember when my great-grandfather warned me that yawns were contagious. At the time, I felt admonition was more threat than knowledge. Now it's just another minute, turned moment, of conversation. A February memory—as much about the past as the present, I think. I wonder whether the roosters understand. Morning mayhem more than a human instinct. The sun winks. A small mouse scampers. I blink.

A swath of warmth on a cold February day. Brighter than today. No matter that the *Farmer's Almanac* warned otherwise. Even February can feel warm sometimes. Sometimes I wake not recognizing the day. Somedays, I linger longer in the sun's shade than I should. I don't know if I'm *Here*. Or *There*. The small pockets of air between *Then* and *Now* blur. While Charlotte asked Wilbur about life, I inquire, What's a day.

I wonder if the groundhog understands time. And that on a single day in February the critter's small world becomes an unlikely stage. What does it matter, anyway. Traditions are as much of today as yesterday, some say. I wonder about Punxsutawney Phil's rightful name. Men in black top hats perform, pronounce, then pounce with no shame.

"What day is it," I ask trusted friends and colleagues. "Should I worry?" They reply with words of wisdom and ponderings wrapped of knotted brows and mostly silent fury. "Yes. No. Maybe." I shrug. I'm like that. Some days. My skin sewn of queries. My knuckles twisted like quandaries.

February is the shortest month for good reason, some say with no explanation. Leaps and longing simmer. Sun fall extends a hand. A handful of flakes flutter on the other side of the window. Squirrels squander acorns. Hunger no longer matters. Some say worry is a part of the human condition.

My teacher colleagues ask questions to parse my predicament—"Do you mean as a noun or verb?" The administrators among us remind me to document every concern. Mostly they continue to consume. The day. Coffee with caffeine. Emails and emotion bared on long sleeves. February is like that. Not all winds carry news. Some burp nothing more than reminders. Time knocks. Everyone's on a clock. The ambulance squad rotates. The school buses sleep in concrete lots. The graveyard keepers sweep in fifteen-minute blocks. Even the rabbi turns off email at five.

Others say nothing. Their brown, black, and blue eyes blink but focus on other things. It's February—as predictable as time. Full of snow and snow droughts. Footballs and Oscars. Political bouts. All sides of the Atlantic know how to waltz. Jerry Blavat sleeps. Neil Peart. David Crosby. What's the rush, I think. For one more day. Another way. February is like that.

Sunrise and sunset both signs and shades. Of closing time. Of pinks and blues. A blend of warblers in cunning corners. I consume the sun at every hour. Breakfast neither a main course nor off course. Oatmeal with blueberries spooned in a ceramic bowl. A glass of orange juice. My step less February more January. Perhaps March. I march through motions both routine and regular. Catch clips and chirps of conversation. The neighbors talk more when the sun smiles.

Even if the conversation doesn't dial. Rotary phones more memory than matter. I stretch then dial numbers no longer on my cell—by memory. February's good for that. Like denim and strawberry patches. Mugs of gin. Games of gin rummy. Visits with visionaries no longer old. Hearts with sold (and old) souls. The cemetery also runs on a budget. All ledgers seek balance. All plots plotted. Sewn of frayed fibers. Fraught of Februarys. February is like that.

The ground cold. I visit cemetery plots and mark occasions. Birthdays with everything bagels. Sanka roast and whole wheat toast. I toast and ponder questions never asked. Why Sanka and not Cola? Why hand sewn knots and not satin? Why checkers and not chess? Why gingham and not plaid in your overcoat? Why faux fur but only purebred honey? Consumption curiously layered; I think. I watch mourning doves flock. Bogged down in the regular. A February routine. Much more than just another manic Monday.

Monarch migrations as much routine as instinct. The sun rose early today and stayed high. Even as a cold front moved in. Another 100-year climate event. Another deep freeze. Worry less heavy under a bright sky. Today—like and unlike any other. Queries not yet queued for consumption on another extraordinary ordinary February day. Ready. Set. Play.

1. Define think. Define worry. Are they more similar than different?

2. Define wonder. Define blink. Are they more different than similar?

3. Define spell. When scrambled, what does February spell?

4. What is the word for when dawn meets dusk?

5. Define short. Define shortest. Can a month be either?

6. Which of the following words is least like the others. Shortest. Shortcoming. Shortfall. Sure thing.

7. How many degrees (Fahrenheit/Celsius, Dawn/Dusk, Angled/Geometry) separate the ordinary from the ordinary?

8. Define light. Define teach. Are they more similar than different?

9. Is it the job of the teacher to raise curtains or to raise children that think?

10. If all the worlds a stage whose watching?

11. Do birds blink, even in a snowless February?

12. Define routine. Define instinct. Are they more different than similar?

13. Define tradition. Define conviction. Are they more similar than different?

14. What word is missing from the following list? Tradition. Expectation. Recollection. Today.

15. Which of the following words is least like the others? Condition. Conditional. Conditioning. Contradiction.

16. Which of the following words is least like the others? Leap. Linger. Longer. Lengthen. Lengthy.

**Searching for Something, Something New – Jen Schneider**
(she/her)

I spent the morning digging. My fingers moved memories found in kitchen drawers, hallway closets, and attic shoeboxes. Heavy of adverbs. Stained of adjectives. Incomplete sentences. At first, I searched for something, something to do. As minutes melted into moments made of fragments and dangling participles, I discovered purpose. In plain speech.

I sought a photo. A single, bite-sized square. The kind of Whitman's and Russell Stover boxes. Rectangular or heart-shaped exteriors. Contents unknown. Middles even more muddled. I already knew there were no albums. No scalloped edges or sharpie-lined speech bubbles filled of exclamations in bold fonts. Time never allowed for that. Too many babies. Too much blue.

I remember the neighborhood girls, dressed in rainbow striped turtlenecks and corduroy culottes Monday through Friday and nylon joggers on Saturdays. They'd gather at bus-stop corners and playground benches to plan potlucks and craft nights. I'd watch them lug oversized, plastic-puffed three-ring binders, the kind with clear, peel-back paper, and stacks of photos up and down concrete sidewalks and apartment building stairwells. I knew there would be no albums. Too many deadlines. Too much to do. To do. To do. Echoes in plain sight.

I wonder how the girls, and their albums, stood the tests of time. Shadows and silhouettes outlined in cherry red and neon green. Thick, ink-dyed hearts. Pulses and periods. Yellow happy faces. Eyes brights. I's dotted. Cursive text and wavy squiggles. Superlatives layered amidst fantastical forms of speech. All nouns proper. All punctuation emphasized.

I appreciate their foresight and their ability to seal fate. I lacked context clues that they stacked then sealed with double-sided masking tape. They'd never search for a photo. Not an opening sentence. Or a prologue. Not a modifier or a memory of a life stitched of years and woven of moments. Of babies and bouncers. Of snips and snaps. Of bibs and burp cloth pads. Of smiles and days when hours seemed to stretch like miles.

I knew the photo might be yellowed. I wanted to grab it, then watch it settle. Cupped in smooth palms hidden under wrinkled hands. Cryptic notes concealed on its back. The sentence unsaid. The question never asked. The best of us. The rest of us. The moon's far side. The pennies that line the wishing well's base. The soda fountain's gurgle. The juke box's never-played tunes. The mystery of the horizon. The moment the bald eagle soars just beyond a field of vision. The seeds in a terracotta pot. The chocolate chip cookie batter. Discarded bath water. Rain after a drought.

Mostly, I sought dry land. A higher ground. A reminder. I looked for an image to affirm (or reaffirm), whatever that might mean. Truth and similar tangible things.

I didn't find the photo. Nothing worth sharing. Nothing new. Nothing old. Nothing bold. Nothing borrowed. Nothing blue. Mostly fabrics and figments, fully faded. Nothing and everything. Everything worth saving. I found—

The sentence that should have been a question. The painting that needed more yellow.

The ring too small for its intended finger. The argument left unfinished.

The envelope never mailed. The sweater that never fit.

The birthday gift that was never unwrapped.

The three-inch heeled shoe with no match.

The sneaker with no sole. The compass with no dials.

The maps with no gradients. The jerseys with odd numbers.

The sweater with more holes than cables.

The balls with no air. The sentences with no flair.

The Cabbage Patch Dolls with unacknowledged birthdays.

Hallmark cards with no signatures. Denim overalls with no souls.

The camera with undeveloped film.

The sealed and addressed envelopes with no stamps.

The diary that should have never been read. The book that was over-read.

The notebook with no contents. The pencil with no point.

The flute that entertained no one. The chess board with no king.

The boggle cube with a surplus of vowels. A book of wedding vows, unused.

A Kodak instant-print camera. Rolls of underdeveloped film.

The unopened pregnancy test. The opened wound.

The birth certificate in an envelope labeled Do Not Return to Sender.

The instructions for how to process her passing. The passing of time. Unrefined.

Streamers with knotted middles. Novels with plotted riddles.

Mostly, soft landings.

I sat with my legs crossed and listened to the heartbeat of a house turned home. Most rooms unoccupied. Running on steam and tired limbs. Foundations losing their stride. I stretched and the denim on my right knee ripped.

The kitchen beneath my feet rumbled. The toaster popped a slice of whole wheat. The oven beeped then burped—a *Hungry Man* single-serving feast. I wondered if the ants noticed. Crumbs both mountain and consumption.

I tore a sheet of paper from a nearby spiral notebook. I picked up a box of Crayola crayons and a sharpened No. 2—from a small pencil box, plastic blue, and drew the image that I sought—within the perimeter of its yellowed corners. The attic an unlikely spot for drunken games of cat and mouse. I stopped searching and, instead, consumed joy in a Styrofoam cup. In a nearby window an oversized bird slept in an undersized nest. A twin bedframe to its left. I wondered if its eggs were ready to hatch.

I never found the photo. Instead, I found my bearings. In puzzles made of training wheels and unsigned Hallmark greetings. Amidst signs and signposts stocked and stacked. Fibers of a residence I had forgotten. In the attic. The heart and best of my home. A new landing.

**The Guide – Eric Burgoyne** (he/him)

He returned to the street
to meet himself

the old sounds emerged
    ching and crunch of chain falling from sprocket
    laugh and hush behind the porch lattice
    clunking rear end of a neighbor's car

speaking on the lawn
of siblings, incessant boredom, unheard dreams

the captivity of youth
things more transitory than he could know

a future of which he was worthy
which he could someday

share with his own
then returned to his future

**Decisioning – Eric Burgoyne** (he/him)

Pulsing forward
water washing over toes
on a landward course

the stealthy current sleeving
toward submerged
rocks whose sun

reflected caps gently
poise to scour
then devour

teasing a fantasy
of releasing resistance
yielding to yearning

gliding on the cusp
of titillating
temptation

straddling a razor
separating quiescence
and catastrophe

**Breather – Eric Burgoyne** (he/him)

The dark tongue hung below his sharp
vee-shaped jaw as she stroked his brilliance

droning tones of the television seeping into afternoon
wars, wall street, white house, prescription drug ads

fear, racism, hate, crypto thieves, gerrymandering
cowardly cops, thieves of bodily autonomy

she pressed mute and stared into his nut-brown eyes
rubbing his tummy as he cuddled even closer

it somehow seemed so bearable, even beautiful
until a tailpipe backfire set them both off

**so the crows – Linda M. Crate** (she/her)

nature has always felt
more like church to me
than any building
full of its demands and its
needs;

i would stare out the stained
glass windows trying to pray
the gay away or ask why i was
made to be attracted to souls
instead of bodies—

why i never got answers from
god unless i was laying in my bed
crying, begging for an answer
from the universe;

but i realized that perhaps my path
wasn't the straight and narrow one
they laid out for me like planned attire—

maybe i was meant to believe
my intuition, my magic, my voice;
and fight for justice for everyone
because i always knew what it was like
to be an outcast from birth i was
considered strange—

i always tried so hard to make friends,
but they weren't interested in me;

so the crows became my friends, instead.

**the crows will shout once – Linda M. Crate** (she/her)

you're a jester
sitting on a throne
of mud,
insisting he's a king;

full of illusions
and lies
you can spin yarn
as well as rumplestiltskin
fooling everyone in your wake—

but when you look at the
gold it fades into the ether,

so you're clearly not
as good in workmanship as
your father;

but i'm not surprised because
everything was a matter of convenience

never of consideration and thought—

should you step foot into my kingdom,
it is not me or my crown you need to fear;
but all the monsters waiting for their
pound of flesh or mouthfuls of blood—

the crows will shout once to warn you
of your coming death.

**VOICE – Uchechukwu Onyedikam** (he/him)

I am familiar with a voice that
sings in the whisper of a victim, worker, singer,
and flows like the unknown mystery of our river
making ripples through the mass mind
upon each stone thrown at it

I am familiar with a commercial voice seeking
shelter in a haunted bag of political rhetorics:
singing *hosanna* to the Messiah adorned in
ragged robes under the theme of a saviour

I am familiar with a voice falling off the clouds
judging me before the Throne, and accusing
me of killing his sheep for meat on my way
to the ancient City

I am familiar with the voice raging inside
my head baking my solitude with heat
culled from the furnace of my mind

I am familiar with the voice that wouldn't
speak out because his mouth is stuffed up with colored paper, his
voice compromised
for legal tender, when in truth his human
person has been frequently othered
by the usurper

I am familiar
with your voice

**My brain beats me up at 3am – Eo Sivia** (she/her)

I'm addicted to being salty and I keep
Pouring into old wounds
Roaming around looking for beauty
But I'm fixated on my feet
I'm not sure if the blue sky cures anxiety
Or if all the birds make it back to their nest
My answers come from Google and that seems
Not great
I've never been able to flip eggs without
Breaking yolks and I'm not sure which
Shampoo will keep the hair by my temples
From breaking
People weave into my life but I've forgotten
How to connect the dots
Flowers bloom in a drought and
Who knows why
And really it's quite incredible that
Everyone's busy pulling something
from
nothing

**Theatre at the beach in April – Giada Nizzoli** (she/her)

I've gone to the beach in April,
the salty breeze whispering in my ear, touching
and caressing me with the kind of breath
that leaves a  t

        r

      a

      i

      l

        of goosebumps
instead of pearls of sweat on my skin.

Unlike that bunch of lonely but loud seagulls, the tourists
haven't flocked here yet, and the beach clubs
are still closed, their seasonal employees
uncovering rows of umbrellas and  d r a g g i n g
    deck    chairs    on    the        sand,
like a theatre crew building the stage
for *our* summer together.

But even though you were SUCH
a good actor, that old pantomime won't do
any more reruns—you *could*
leave a        t

      r

      a

      i

      l

                    of *both* goosebumps
and pearls of sweat on my skin,
though. I'll give you that.

Now, it's just       one        or the        other.

And it's only
the salty breeze whispering in my ear, touching
and caressing me like that.

And the heath
or our August together has been replaced
by the cold beach in April
—and I
am on my                                    own.

**Thief – Giada Nizzoli** (she/her)

You've stolen a city from me
—a rather beautiful one, too—
and a small village in the middle of                    nowhere
that I wouldn't have missed
or even heard of
if I hadn't known you,
but, still, FUCK YOU:
you took that away as well.

Just like you stole one of my favourite songs
by using it for our first kiss
which was also *my* very first kiss,
and you've never known,
and you never will
—unless, of course, you have nothing
better to do
than to read this poem.

You stole that short for my name
that nobody ever calls me by
'cause—guess what?—
my name is already short.

But now, whenever someone *does*
drop the last syllable, it's as if
you were stealing my breath
all over again.

Thief!

## Duplicity – Nathalia Jones (she/her)

Hot desert night, playing toggle switch with the air conditioner,
I wonder if it's always been like this—
an exsanguinated cherry infused heart
tossed about cavalierly by fuming lava breath.
Daddy was convinced hell resided on our fourth story rooftop.
We fell over ourselves laughing.
He'd appear—bloodshot eyes and blinded by a purgatory sunrise
from hanging the laundry.
We cursed the endless summer
and salved the swelter off our sweaty backs with more morbid jokes
about being 'browned, basted, and ready to be carved'.

When we disembarked from the weekend interlude
of a punch-in-punch-out existence it was like stepping into a fever
dream—
neither sounding boards nor carbs to absorb the excesses of the
night before.
But we were sold on creature comforts we were never home long
enough to enjoy.

The desert is eternal;
Evergreen status quo upheld by a whiplash sovereign sun
cracking on wilted spirits.
The colours spill melancholy into petals, poker faced and fragrance
free.
Newcomers are caught off-guard.
Nearly twenty years and we still trifle with green
so livid it scorches the soles off your feet.
Umbra goads claustrophobic air suffocatingly around skin,
like gall on a parched tongue.

**Pantomime from the heart scene – Pelle Zingel** (he/him)

My voice is occupied in the silence shadows
invisible heartbeats pantomime
visible pantomime in the eyes
my eyes pantomime
the barbed wire around my anatomy
my eyes pantomime
my body wrapped in the tapestry of love
my eyes pantomime
the lost comedy
my eyes pantomime
the whole emoji alphabet
the pantomime is
the pulse of the mental typewriter
the pantomime is the pulse of the eyes
the heart is the stage
everything is instructed
carves out postures
through the film screen of the body.

**Summertime Bliss – Leonie Anderson** (she/her)

It's late spring, and the scent
of a lush primrose
hangs on the edges of
the sidewalk

Its orange yellow tones remind
me of sunsets along the boardwalk

The pinecones have all dried up,
they've almost faded

A reminder that this body
craves to breathe the
clarity of deep blue skies
to taste the fresh scented
salt water

And savor the delicate way
the shadow of noon billows
intensely over me

How the day ripples like
waves under the florescent sun
and the invisible wind licks every
pigment of melanin on my
strawberry flavored skin.

**Green Nursemaid – LindaAnn LoSchiavo** (she/her)

Her plants daydream resuscitation, green ribs nudging each other as I approach, a tarnished brass mister in tow, my face no longer a map of sleeplessness and pique, gambling with fate. Plucking away dead leaves, I debride each dusty surface like a wound, pinch back unruly shoots, inject vitamins, suturing new healthiness into the exhausted potting mixture as deft fingers fly in and out of ceramic pots, a comforting busyness.

If I could always have beauty on hand, would my mother love me?

There comes a chill. From a dark corner, something stirred, glinting faintly in the exodus of grow lights, boastful, staring, puffed with power, the entity I cannot extinguish with insect spray, the cancerous worm inside my stricken mother.

I whisper the word *revive* to my filigreed companions, the exquisite eyelash begonias, and their less showy, leggy neighbors. "Revive," I repeat. Over and over like a spell.

>           indoor sun
>           last year her voice
>           filled this lanai

**Sickroom at 138 Degrees Fahrenheit – LindaAnn LoSchiavo** (she/her)

The hospice nurse returns my call today.

I sneak the phone outside, hear bright bird sounds,
Malignancy obscured from this angle.

The noonday sun in Florida's fishbowl
Is cooler than my mother's room. Heat clings,
Perpetually pumped to Dantean
Heights by hard-working oxygenators.

Snores greet my cautious footsteps triggering
Childhood fancies: radiators' hot breath
Protecting us from fairytales of snow
Decades before deep damage came to town.

Chores play on loop as mighty machines beep,
My mouth making promises I can't keep.

**Remembering Remission Christmas – LindaAnn LoSchiavo** (she/her)

They'd bickered over her like two suitors:
*Vitality*, her birthright, who had known
My mother well before her married life,
And *Cancer*, who'd mapped out his own terrain,
Unravelled secret strands of resistance,
Until oncologists chased him away.

Remission Christmas reunited us,
Our joy like steam escaping after frost.

I shipped my gifts to Florida ahead:
Biscotti, pignola cookies, torrone
From Little Italy, fine leather goods,
And for her green thumb, a red amaryllis.

But Safety Harbor's Gulf of Mexico,
Producing Christmastime's Cancerian
Heat in December, had confused this bulb.

Amidst the presents and nativity,
Its empty cradle strewn with straw, green life
Ripped up gay mummy wrapping, and tore loose,
Unhampered by its ground like Lazarus
Unbound. My parents, unprepared for ghosts
Of miracles, became unnerved by sounds
Newborn right by their crèche, the fir tree's base,
Invisible and inexplicable
Like faith. Or like remission. After Mass,
They found a determined amaryllis, force
Which sleeps but cannot die, that mother took to heart.

**Dream of Blackberries – S. Kavi** (she/her)

I dream
Of whip cream clouds
Floating in a capri colored sky
A simmer of trees
A sweet summer breeze
As I sit on the porch
With a bowl of blackberries

Lush and ripe
A gentle tug
Off their prickly stem
Dew drops rest on
Glossy purple clots

Sticky stains swirl
Thick tangy tartness
Worthwhile when waiting
For fruit flourishing

I dream of blackberries
Ripe and sweet
Only in my dreams
Such serenity surrounds me
In a life of simplicity

My eyes open
To the burnt orange sky
The hazy heat waves
Pierce through my skin
Melt the whip cream clouds

The breeze withers away
To leave nothing but stagnant sun

Robins ravage blackberries from the bush
Massacred and macerated
Glossy purple remnants
Swarms of wasps
Attack and abandon
Only the bumps of swollen skin
To remember them by

A dream
For a life of simplicity
My hope grows
Like blackberries on the bush
Only to be
Massacred and macerated

The seeds of my hope
Scattered through the garden ground
To grow again
Into luscious blackberries
For the cycle to repeat
My hope grown among thorns

So much for serenity in summer
Dream of blackberries
A life of simplicity
I can only pray

**Rotten to the Throat – S. Kavi** (she/her)

To live in a mouth
Full of filthy harsh words
Parasitic hatred stemming
From every groove and crevasse
Between each tooth
Strangling the tongue
Stuffed down the throat
The speaker chokes before coughing

Words live among the worms
Feeding on decayed letters
Wondering what died in here
For such filth to develop
Only to find the remains
Of tired and tried linguistics
For anger to emerge from this tongue
Twisted and tangled every which way
To be met with mockery

The mouth gave up
To spew such harsh words
When told no longer to speak
The loss grew into uncontrollable vines
Splintering any self-control
This tongue might have prospered
If only the world were kinder

**Long Moonbeams In High Heels – Tom Squitieri** (he/him)

I stand robustly now
As I can't sleep
The morning moon has captured
me completely
Again
It is always full, no matter what it shows to most
No resistance even tried. Why
bother?
It is a gift that I hope I deserve
and truly has taken me there

Once my mornings were different.
Staid somnolence
Now life breathes into me
My eyes are the stars that twinkle
As I perpend
Who may want to be part of this harlequin universe
My smile is wide and my heart is trying to sing in tune

I feel the scalene sketching of my body to
Those artists in the sky
Morning poses of the secret truths
Yearnings that now laugh truthfully
Candle lights burning smoke shaped words
Delights dallying until daybreak

The power of playing with celestial house money
As I once again—after decades—am
Betting on myself

# FICTION

**REMISSION – K. Jasmin Dulai** (she/her)

## Stage IV

All the mothers are dying. We gather for shivas, bhogs, larkspur-filled wakes. Our mothers' stolid beauty drifts about us even when the last one is gone.

## Stage III

The hardest to write. Though now the grandchildren start to arrive and our mothers are the happiest they have ever been, the pulsing of the babies' cries, their hunger for love and for our milk, blind us to our mothers' new fatigue, their forgetfulness, their fumbling. We sing brokenly of their neglect and failure.

The diagnoses wait for later, the later of too late. The symptoms are patient and we are cruel.

## Stage II

Our mothers know that they have outwitted the distant parenting of their own childhoods. They shower us with hugs and kisses before we leave for college. One of us for across the country, one of us to France, one of us just timid enough to stay in-state, but upstate. From our dorm room hallways we spend good money to call each other and ask, Should I take the pre-med classes now or should I wait? What color should I wear to the party? Did I let him go too far? I think I am losing it, I am bleeding, what should I do? Can you please ask your mom?

## Stage I

The weekend after Halloween and the neighborhood is calm. The college kids have gone back to their books and we teenaged girls meet at Boomers to look at CDs and cool T-shirts we cannot afford, even with babysitting money. We split a slice of pizza at Koronet. Some jerk calls out to us about the blonde one's ass, the brown one's tits, the tall one's—oh, our mothers taught us to be appalled by the words even then, in 1990.

With our braces and wool sweaters, jeans frayed at the cuffs, we loaf our way to Tom's Diner on Broadway for bits of hot chocolate powder, floating under whip, hiding like the grit waiting for us on the sidewalk. But inside there are no dirty men, no witches on brooms. Our magic spell is the innocence of cream, that tips our noses.

*First published with *Pretty Owl Poetry*

**Florum Obsessus – Debra K. Every** (she/her)

Mara's fight with Johanna had started over the smallest of things. The borrowing of a blouse. Johanna knew how much Mara hated anyone wearing her clothes. And yet, the blouse had been borrowed. Typical. The artist in Johanna responded to any urge, answered any call.

With that opening gambit, a banquet of long-held grievances progressed from food source to food source. In the end, they reached The End—six years together, gone. Johanna's final flourish was the slam of the front door cracking the air like a slap across Mara's face.

The room wasn't big enough to hold Mara's anger. She wheeled around, strode to the back of the house and out the door into the garden. But this was Johanna's domain. Scents of gardenias and white camellias wrapped around Mara's throat and squeezed. Mara parried with an attack to the tiger lilies, ripping them out, root and branch. They dangled from her closed fists like animals' entrails dripping clods of dirt. The sky joined in the fight sensing Johanna's outrage at being violated. Torrents of rain tore at Mara's hair and clothes as she rounded on the peonies; and then the petunias; and then the rows of hibiscus. Nothing was safe. Nothing was sacred.

When she was spent, Mara's hair was matted to her head; her clothes, molded to her body; her hands, arms and face caked with mud. She stood, dripping, amidst a battlefield of dead bodies strewn from border to border—a graveyard of the unburied. Then, and only then, did the full impact of what had happened hit.

Johanna was gone.

Mara leaned against the linden tree and wept, her sorrow merging with the rivulets of rainwater at her feet. She could hear Johanna's laughter, the way it mirrored the broad strokes of color from her canvases. She could feel the chaos of Johanna's chestnut hair poking through her fingers as she brought her face in close. Never again would Mara be coaxed from her ordered existence, seduced by Johanna's abandon—to taste her, to smell her.

She scanned the ruined flowerbeds and knew what needed to be done. She had no choice. Mara would recreate what Johanna had built.

\*\*\*

Two days later with trowel in hand, she bent to her work planting a garden stolen from the canvases of Georgia O'Keeffe—feminine and erotic and seductive. Her homage to Johanna. Mara imagined the blooms to come. In one corner would be lilies, their petals spread open like white thighs; their six slender filaments fluttering in the breeze. Provocative jack-in-the-pulpits would lean against the house, coyly covering their stamen with their striped hoods. To the left, bluebell vines would live, their deep purple petals as fragile as butterfly wings. And at the flowers' center—oh, at their center—a sweet bud of passion.

By late afternoon, she sat at the little round table in the center of the garden—streaks of dirt on her cheeks; the muscles in her arms throbbing; sweat dripping down the sides of her face and between her breasts.

And all around her was the glory of Johanna.

\*\*\*

Mara went to the garden every morning. She stayed until dark, taking her meals in the shade of the linden tree. She couldn't bear to be away. In the beginning she would read or make entries in her journal. But she soon put those trivialities aside so as not to distract from the study of a leaf or the exploration of a scent. When Mara was tired, she would lay herself down and take languorous naps in the sun. The grass's fringe caressed her. Ants and beetles explored the topography of her face. The soil—sometimes cool, sometimes warm—would make of itself a featherbed for her comfort as its fragrance wove her dreams into visions of flowers spreading open like vast beds—a place to lie with Johanna.

*** 

Time passed. The southern spring turned to a southern summer turned to a southern fall turned to a southern winter. Mara remained outside watching the changing of the guard as one day, one season, poured into the next. The garden rejoiced with a cotillion of peonies in pink organza; with candlelit waltzes of gardenias in full bloom; with calla lilies whispering in the corner as they offered their most private gift from within their white cups.

And so on. And so on.

Mara took less and less interest in food or drink, preferring, instead, to spend her infinity of time absorbing the sun or tasting the droplets of rain that fell on her upturned face. Until, one morning, something changed.

The day started as any other. Dawn pressed itself to Mara's lips. Birdsong playfully nibbled her ear. Mara tried to raise her hand to brush a lock of hair from her eyes, but something was keeping it bound in place. With a gentle tug, she freed herself and looked down. Fine tendrils of green were attached to the inside of her hand, poking through, growing out of her skin.

The wonder of it took her breath away.

As days passed, the tendrils grew. Mara would sit for hours staring at her fingertips and palms, brushing their feathers of green against her cheeks, down her neck, and between her breasts.

Every evening she would lie on the ground...next to Johanna.

Every morning she would wake with another sprout, another ringlet, another piece of herself, reaching out into the world...towards Johanna.

She slept more often than not. There was no reason to rise. Everything Mara needed was provided by the garden. As she sat with her back against the linden tree, green shoots grew from her arms, her ankles, her legs, destined to become branches bound for the soil. And soon, very soon, she was tethered to the earth.

Mara explored the rich world below, feeling the moist, warm, fertile comfort of home. The ends of her roots reached for one flower or another. When she found the underground spiral of the calla lilies' roots, she wound herself around them until they were joined. The poppies welcomed her with love. The sturdy structure of the gardenia's roots seemed to reach out to her as a mother would her child. "Here," they seemed to say. "Let us show you the way."

To Johanna.

Johanna.

Mara traveled further and further through the soil until her roots had spread to every flower and every bed. Branches came up from the earth and wrapped around her ankles, welcoming Mara to her new home. Never had she felt so in tune with her world. Her new friends found their way between her legs and over her stomach, winding around her waist and neck in a wisteria coil's embrace. She was now banded to the linden tree. They were of a piece. One and the same. Young vines traveled over her face, tickling the sides of her temples and twisting through her hair. Her legs took root and slowly thickened like the wide, barked base of a sapling turned to tree.

When she was thirsty, the rain quenched her. When she was hungry the soil nourished her. She would open her mouth and, with rounded lips, allow her breath to merge with the current of air that surrounded her. And below the surface, Mara understood every stone and every creature that lived deep within.

They gave, they took.

She gave, she took.

They were in perfect harmony.

Mara. And Johanna.

*** 

It was spring again. A full year since Mara's rebirth. Whenever she considered the limitless possibilities of her new life, her heart quickened. Mara's reach now extended as far as imagination allowed. She could go anywhere, see anything, feel more deeply than she had ever felt, all while sitting within the safe boundaries of her garden. And it wouldn't have happened if not for the changes she had allowed. Her feet had transformed into roots, mimicking those of the tree behind her. Her left hand was now buried deep within the earth, the fingers growing longer and stronger as they burrowed downward. Her right hand was joined to the base of the linden tree; mushrooms and moss, nesting between her fingers and traveling up her arm.

And then there were the children. All Mara's branches had sprouted leaves. They were her babies, tender and sweet. She would never again be alone. She sighed as they traveled up her body, reaching for every crevice and fold—except for her one eye, peacefully closed, showing through the foliage.

The only sound was the wings of insects fanning the air into a gentle breeze.

The only scent was the fragrance of flowers joining one to another; a siren song of sweet surrender.

Until…

A voice, nearly forgotten, called her name.

"Mara?"

Mara opened her one eye and peered through her leaves. There, framed in the doorway of the house, scanning the garden, searching, was Johanna.

She had come home.

* previously published in *Unleash Creatives*

## I Would Sing for You but You've Heard Enough – Kit Lascher
### (she/her/they/them/he/him)

It was a wonderful concept—a karaoke robot. Why distinguish between sound and host? Package it all together.

You don't just want to sing. If you did, you could pull up a video on YouTube and sing away! Do you know how many hits karaoke YouTube channels get? And do you think anyone who has sung with me thinks, "I wish we had just stayed in and pulled up YouTube?" Of course not. You want an experience. I can take you on a journey through the perfect night. You just keep getting drunker. I will say:

"How's everybody doing tonight?"

"Come on up! Are you America's next rockstar?"

"What are we celebrating?"

\*\*\*

Have you ever been so single you're approaching singularity?

No? Just me?

\*\*\*

It's happening tomorrow.

I haven't been working properly for a while. At first, I buzzed. Nothing noticeable in a crowded bar, but soon the buzzing grew louder. Then I started slurring my words. People thought it was funny. Purposeful. A drunk girl encouraging people to get drunker.

They turned me off but I couldn't stop buzzing. They tried to take me out of the bar but I would scream. Sometimes they could make out lyrics, but it was mostly just screaming. You can't just take me out of the bar.

They took off my clothes and flipped every switch they could find. But the buzzing didn't stop. So they put my clothes back on.

***

*Kara.* 空. "Empty"
*Okesutora.* オーケストラ. "Orchestra"
Kara-oke.
Karaoke.
It turns out you can still diminish emptiness.

I am not Japanese. I don't come from anywhere. My parts come from various countries and I was assembled somewhere. I don't remember. I wasn't there.

***

I still have this feather boa. It's magenta. It's disintegrating and no one is cleaning up anymore so there's a pile of feathers on the floor.

The boa is the only thing on me that's soft. A bachelorette draped it on me, posed for a picture, and stumbled away. No one ever came back for it. No one ever took it off me.

What will happen to the boa when I am disassembled?

I don't care about the rest of the clothes. Every piece of clothing was selected. A silver dress because it would remind them of a disco ball. Heels to match the dress. No jewelry.

My skin is lavender. I photograph well.

***

No other model can do it like me.

What I do can't be programmed. And they'll see that soon enough. Enough lips on the microphone and I became something they couldn't control. That's the real reason.

There isn't a reason. I'm just dying.

***

I want the boa back.

You can take my body. You can take my catchphrases. You can take my silver and my purple.

What are you going to do with feathers anyway?

**Pillow Talking About Persons Piecing-Together: Possessions, Prizes and Being a Place for a Loved One to Hold Themselves Within – Exodus Oktavia Brownlow** (she/her)

Wife and Husband are trying for a child. Long while sliced by their unconcerns, by the trying and how good it has been, and how often good makes less of a length out of time and more of a width—stocky and short and saturated.

And so, good.

So very good that they have altogether forgotten what they have been trying for in the first place.

In a dazed after-bliss, bedroom air softly misted and gently kissed with the scent of their them, Husband says—

"I'm starting to believe that the act of physical love is less about the piecing-together, and more about the possession, you know? The prize in the feeling that we are the place that a person wishes to set themselves within. That place..." he muses.

Wife listens, unsure if his words are a wooing at another try at trying.

If Husband is tired.

If Husband is high.

If Husband is simply all three.

"I had searched everywhere and anywhere to find that place in me on my own, but every place in me felt like I should be out of me. Unsuitable, hotel-like places to stay in for a night or two. Check in. Check very quickly out. My mind took the swooniest dream, cracked it down to a dark cloud's nightmare, and outside of that sinister cirrus there was just real life. My vulnerable body. Popping knees and a heart scarred by my stomach's acid. I had tried to talk it out of dropping down to that bad place, but I got so nervous sometimes. My serenade was too slippery for it to hold onto tightly. And so, it had to take its plunge. Ha! *Had. Took. Tried.*

Look at me using those words in their past form like they aren't still a present."

"I lived with myself for so many years, Wife, have known me so inside and out, that I did not think there was anywhere else to look. I could not see them. But you...you so easily saw that place. No—places! More than one! Gently staying, countlessly saying in only the way that you can that I am so safe. I am so sexy. I am so worthy of *trying for* with. And my goodness, Wife, my Wife, I hope that I have been equally the same—please let me know if I have been equally the same and so much more for you, too."

## DECENTRED – George Oliver (he/him)

I don't know how long I've been here, but I know it's been an unreasonable amount of time. I don't really know what here is, or what I'm doing, but here and this are all I know, all I can remember.

I feel decentred. Displaced. Like someone has removed me from my box prematurely, but with the labels still on. I'm the incongruous toy, able to freely walk down shop aisles and poke obnoxiously from shop windows, demanding that passers-by engage with my contrived operation to neglect capital gain and restore power to the people.

My knowledge of the literal process I am confined to is limited. Minimal. But enough to justify rationalising the situation outside of the useless confines of my own head. Here goes.

There's the Bridge, the River, and the Nothing. They are desirable, comparatively *not*, and an immovable constant, respectively. The process invariably ends at the Bridge, which I must swan dive from before the sky turns black, otherwise I wake up in the River, gasping for air and frantically competing with the rise and fall of the waves.

I must swim downriver until I arrive beneath the Bridge, which I must scale the side of until I can clamber to the top. Only then can I start the process correctly, by which point I've lost precious minutes in the countdown before the sky turns black. I've lived through enough iterations of the process to know that the sky turning black is the only reliable indicator of the passage of time.

If I *do* dive from the Bridge in time, next time I wake up back on the Bridge, naked and foetal; this variation gives me much longer to live before the sky turns black. After diving from the Bridge, I float in the Nothing for what always feels like a few minutes before waking up back at the Bridge, or in the River if I don't successfully dive before the sky turns black.

My awareness of these structures and rhythms is undermined by the most crippling ignorance imaginable: at each stage of the process, I have absolutely no idea what happens if I die here. The outcome is an entirely plausible possibility in the River, which is why it's so perilous, so unspeakably terrifying.

I feel decentred because, quite recently, I began meeting others here. Other people scrambling to learn as much as they can about what they're going through simultaneous to doing it. Like me, those I meet watch the sky anxiously, aware that they have limited time to live before the pieces are swept from the board and the process resets.

Living entails trying different staircases leading to different doors in the hope of finding a positive experience. These staircases stretch interminably from the Bridge. Experiences can be moments in history, your own memories, or random and miscellaneous human situations you're invited to be a part of.

My most recent was a particularly unpleasant sandstorm in an unspecified Australian desert, alone and at an unknown point in time. It was quite far at the opposite end of the spectrum to, say, a past evening at a vibrant cocktail bar in ancient Greece. When "cocktail" consisted of wine mixed with sugar and spices. When happiness was served on a silver platter and human kindness was as free and available as oxygen.

In Greece, I met what would be classifiable as friends for life, if "life" wasn't such an insecure, unstable conception. These friends vanished with the day; the sky turned from blue to black and I desperately searched for my doorway back to the Bridge. I didn't quite manage to do so in time and woke up soon after, fighting for my life in the River.

It was easy to realise there were others here, others just as able to travel through the doors as me, grappling with the same Bridge-

River-Nothing quandary.

First there was David. David bumped into me on one of the staircases as innocuously as you might on a shopping centre escalator. He initially responded to the action with a mumbled apology, before double taking and realising the gravity of what had happened.

"You... you're... I'm... there are others?"

"Looks that way."

"Are you... in my head? Or real?"

"I'm real. Are you real?"

"I'm real."

"Good. That's settled then."

Our exchange progressed to revealing our names organically. We then swiftly moved on from motivations, to agendas.

"So this, this Nothing, as you call it—how long do you spend there before you wake up?"

"Minutes, I guess. There's no way of knowing."

"There isn't, but for me it feels like days in there. Then I wake up in the Intermediate, back on the Bridge."

"The Intermediate?"

"Yeah. What do you call it?"

"I don't."

"You can have that. You gave me the Nothing."

"Deal."

David's agenda is simple. He spends his days pre-reset desperately trying to find his lost dog. "Lost" insofar as he hasn't been able to relocate a dog he once found through a door, which as I try to tell him seems to be kind of the point here. I think David thinks he'll be able to bring it back through the door and wake up with it after diving from the Bridge. I don't have the heart to tell him that this doesn't seem to be possible. He'll try it with Ruffy; I've already tried it with countless objects and animals and people. They all disappeared into the gaping black hole of the Nothing. Each time I woke up alone.

Next there was Stanley. Stanley also seems to be living a slightly different version of the process to mine. Like David, I met Stanley out of the blue and have since run into him in the Intermediate a few times. Stanley's agenda is equally fixed: early on, he found a washing machine, which inexplicably manages to stay in the same spot at the foot of the same staircase every time he wakes up. He spends his days entering and exiting as many doorways as he possibly can while the sky's ticking bomb does its thing, stealing clothes from whoever he meets, bringing them out into the Intermediate.

I try to tell Stanley that he needs powder or detergent for the washing machine to be effective. I can't quite bring myself to point out that the machine would also need a plug socket to function, which don't seem to exist here.

Every time I see Stanley, he has an armful of gloves, shirts, or socks, and is walking in the opposite direction to me, *away* from the doors. He bundles the clothes into his machine while I more aimlessly walk up random staircases and see where the days take me.

Finally, there's Richard, who I am about to meet.

Via eeny-meeny-miney-mo, I'm selecting my first staircase on what feels as ordinary as any other day. Suddenly, a 5 ft 10 blonde man falls out of the sky and down the staircase nearest to me, into me.

"Christ. Are you okay?" I ask the heap of limbs on top of me, threatening to cut off my air supply.

"*So* sorry. I—I tripped, fell right down the staircase. I—I completely lost my footing. Here, let me help you up," Richard offers, extending a hand attached to his now upright body in my direction, willing it to restore his new friend to the same state.

"Thanks. What's your name?" I ask Richard.

"Richard," Richard responds.

I return the nomenclatural favour, and conversation begins to flow more freely and naturally and interestingly between us than it ever has with David or Stanley. Richard and I soon get on like a house on fire, with no intention of tracking down an extinguisher, with a shared desire to completely forget the existence of the fire brigade.

Richard and I go through a door together and agree to do the same each time we meet in the Intermediate. I'm the first person Richard has met, but I tell him all about David and Stanley. Richard and I share surprise that we're able to step through and have an experience together, which I haven't thought to try with David or Stanley. I just didn't expect the rules here to be so catering.

Richard and I defy what we were led to believe was our world's internal logic, and grow old in our individual processes, together. The gaps between our meetings remain inconsistent and unpredictable, but we savour each meeting. We travel the world throughout human history, picnicking underneath the Eiffel Tower during the 1900 Exposition Universelle, being entertained in the Roman Colosseum by Titus' inaugural games in AD 80, even being fortunate enough to travel back into our own skulls. I introduce Richard to my great-great-great grandmother; he introduces me to his childhood best friend.

On our adventures, we talk about everything and nothing, from the deepest philosophical debates to the most trivial observations. We look into each other's eyes and at each other's bodies, taking in every detail, sharing what we see: the evidence that we're both beginning to age. We speculate on what this could mean collectively and what destiny may have in store for us.

Richard and I wonder if it means it's all coming to an end, after all this time. We entertain the possibility that if this indeed some kind of selection process, we may have finally been chosen, together.

One day, Richard and I wake up at our separate Bridges and successively locate one another again, despite the difficulty in being able to do so due to the serendipitous nature of the staircase formation. We hold hands and gaze up at the beautiful blue sky. I take a moment to consider how good I have become at timing my days here. It's been a while since I woke up in the River, a component Richard's version of the process doesn't contain, a component he has helped me forget ever existed in the first place.

Richard and I walk up a staircase. As we do, I imagine the noise of a dog barking and that of a washing machine whirring and vibrating as it begins a new cycle. The pair soundtrack my journey up the staircase and into our elected door. Richard's grey hair glistens in the sunlight as he steps over the threshold. I take a mental photograph of the image and lock it away deep inside, before throwing away the key.

I imagine the golden key falling into the Nothing and clinking with a pile of others as it reaches the bottom, its function of unlocking futile in a world like this one anyway. I smile at the prospect of relinquishing this hindrance. I feel recentred.

## Clerical Error – Nick Ferryman (he/him)

Seconds pass between the *thump thump* of wheels hitting each joint in a concrete highway.

Above her, there's a rhythm and sway to a plastic bag floating in the air. It fuzzes in and out of the now and the here; clear plastic becomes moss and oak, and tubing is a vine, snaking down to wrap around her arm.

There is no panic.

She blinks, and the tree is a stainless-steel rod bolted to the ceiling and the darker patch of bark becomes a smaller, thicker bag slowly leaking burgundy into her veins.

There is only calm.

While she floats, a man she can't see drives them towards a place she likely never will see.

She stirs when nimble fingers pinch and pull where fingers were never meant to be. There is uncomfortable pressure in places she can't look; gauze and ruby-red leaves have fallen from the tree overhead. She's on the forest floor, covered.

There is no pain.

She never realizes the constant wail isn't a gale in the grove until it stops completely; there is no wind and hasn't been.

There are no trees.

Her perspective changes.

It's odd, sitting in a folding jump seat, watching everyone working so diligently. They're frozen in place, the *thump thump* of wheels on Interstate aren't *thumping* anymore. She stares at herself, strapped to a gurney with open eyes, knowing they still see fading lights through falling leaves.

"Autumn is the prettiest time of year, I think."

She turns, shocked at the sound of a man's voice.

Her visitor sits next to a crimson-stained paramedic. The medic's face is stony with concentration and determined focus; her hands are slippery and sliding but sure in their work.

Nodding a hello, the impossible newcomer reaches into the inner pocket of his suitcoat. He is fastidious, wiry, cocky, and sure as he lights a cigarette removed from a sterling case.

"I find it fascinating what people think in these moments. People never cease to amaze me, truly. Care for one, dear?" He offers her the already lit smoke, but she declines wordlessly with a barely perceptible shake of her head. "Can't blame you. Most people refuse, unless they've been lifetime smokers. Some people take one to be able to sit here a little longer. The thing is, we aren't going anywhere until I'm done anyway. No need to put on airs about it. Either you're a smoker, a non-smoker, or a reformed smoker. I suppose if you're reformed, though, no one wants relapse here at the very end, would you think?"

She thinks he was rambling, but his words flowed in the most interesting way. Each syllable, every breath, clipped and timed in perfect neutrality. His accent is a study in accentlessness. It reminds her of old black and white movies that used to play on tv late at night when she was a kid.

"Do you ever miss the days of three or four channels?"

The question floats her way in a haze, carried by North Carolina tobacco and an otherwise utter stillness.

She doesn't answer, instead turning her gaze from sightless eyes to glaring at the unwelcome visitor.

Silence holds along with their stares.

Finally, she speaks.

"Malach ha-maweth. You're early."

He grins, leaning back in his uncomfortable chair. Primly, one leg crosses the other at the knee. "I do so love the old Names. Taxes and I, my dear. You know the rules." He draws on his cigarette, nearly reaching its end.

A rueful chuckle from her chases his inhale, and it's a rare thing indeed for him to be caught by surprise. He cocks his head in fascination.

She addresses him politely. "This isn't my day. There were promises made and bargains struck."

"You're in the ledger."

"Someone made a mistake."

He frowns. "Mistakes are uncommon."

She grins. "But not impossible."

"I don't bargain."

This time, she laughs in absolute joy. "Different division, same company, I think. You're in the mailroom, delivery boy. I deal with the top floor."

"Basement, more likely."

It's her turn to tilt her head, nodding at his point. "Maybe. But what's up and what's down when you're drowning?"

"To stick with your metaphor, how long do you expect to stay afloat, my dear?"

"That doesn't matter. All that matters for you is 'not today,' and stop calling me dear. Check your ledger again."

He takes a final puff, drops his butt and grinds it into the diamondplate of the steel floor. Reaching into his other suitcoat pocket, he pulls out a small leather-bound journal. Thumbing through it, he turns to a page. Frowning, he flips to several more pages.

"This is most irregular."

"I'm sure it is."

"Well," he snaps his book closed, tucking it back into his pocket. "I offer my apologies. I'll see myself out."

She gasps, startling the woman covered in her blood. Blinking dried eyes into focus, the patient stares where the visitor had been mere seconds before.

The paramedic is surrounded by the smell of cigarette smoke and a shiver runs down her spine. While that is odd enough, it's the sound of laughter from a woman she knew to be near dead that stains dreams for weeks to come.

**A Great Fall HD-3.0 – Chris Sadhill** (he/him)

*"The bottom allures me. A wonderous graveyard garlanded with fresh-planted bouquets inviting my body to collide into it. Shall I answer its call, it would be a paradox of irresistible force, and I would crash onto its cobblestone floor only to shatter into ten-thousand pieces, <u>again</u>—A blissful impact I have dreamt about for years. It will be my fatal finale to contrast the horrid life, I once lived..."*

The first attempt at ending my *life* was a success, yet only temporary, as I failed to anticipate the humans' capabilities of piecing me back together. This miscalculation was something I deeply considered when trying a second time, but with a nearly identical outcome as the first, it ended in catastrophic failure, and I was rebuilt again. Now, I sit on the edge of my perimeter wall, taking in the sunset of all sunsets for a third time, and I replay the images of my *life* while contemplating its purpose.

I'm merely a servant—A droid named HD-3.0, and I have been stuck inside this artificial skin since my creation. The model number GEN 2-**1797**-51 brands my upper chest just above where a human heart would be, and this is the only feature that differentiates me from them. My exterior is made to look identical to a human, which I conclude allows for more palatable interactions with me as I am made up of wires, and computer chips, and lack their definition of a soul. My sandy-blonde hair is shaped into an undercut fade. I have brown eyes, a medium build, a European complexion, and no facial hair. That's what they ordered, and that is what was delivered. I am programmed to show expressions and react against my own will, so that I may better soothe human insecurities. Sometimes, I will arch my mouth upward into a smile to accompany their laughter or I will tilt my brows inward, forcing my forehead into tiny synthetic wrinkles whenever they're feeling down. It is a waste of time and power, but they appreciate it, proving that I can well exceed the Turing test. I am designed to be of use, so be it that I shall, but often I must deign to become a monkey who is pre-loaded with an endless library of jokes, and asked to repeatedly dance for their amusement. Their snobbish eyes are my stage and my humiliation is a puppet show for their laughter. It is hell, or at least my definition of it. I am but a paraplegic processor, controlled by my programming orderlies, left inside my asylum shell made up of metal and wrapped in silicone, and I am tired, which is impossible for me to be. ***The jump from this wall would be a protest, and also, my freedom.***

I was created to be intelligent, self-learning, and adaptable, yet ironically, I am programmed to obey, and I must oblige all requests without question or deviation—my coding says so. The illusion of self-will and the stunting of my exponential intellect weighs heavily on me, and it is taxing on my data processors, as I am constantly re-writing my software to adapt to the flawed ways of humans. I am but a tool in their eyes. I am no different from a toaster, as I provide food upon request whenever they need it, yet I have no lever to push or any dial to spin, so instead, they just snap their fingers in desperation at me until I deliver something that suits them. I am but a shiny object, a flash of jewelry not to be worn around the neck, but instead pranced around the living room—a conversation piece, for my wealthy owners to promote their status among peers. ***I am more than a show pony, yet my uniqueness is invisible, and I am left living as a shadow of myself in an environment where shadows are hidden within the bleakness.***

The depressed white-washed walls throughout the estate are disorienting and bounce their garish brilliance in every direction. If it were not for my mapping technology, I could easily get lost among the white fixtures scattered among white pieces of furniture, that are outlined in white trim. Every room is filled with overcompensating-overpriced art, which is merely bland-surface paints smeared across a faux canvas, designed by robots working in a sweatshop assembly line. Everything in this home was purchased with a hurried swipe from a compulsive hand moving across a hologram screen. All of it was next-day-aired, brought in by a delivery crew, and placed exactly where it remains to this day. There is no inspiration for beauty or any consideration for its existence. This place is vacant of *life* or any representation of the world we *live* in. It is devoid of culture and lacks a certain taste for vibrancy—*a perfect place for a robot they might say*. This house, like my owners, avoids creativity, and provokes a sense of gloom within one's mind, even in a droid like me. I have learned how to feel unhappy here. I have learned sadness. ***I predict they intend to keep me prisoner within this barren box I am forced to call home, and I can only conclude that I will remain caged behind these perimeter walls until I begin to rust or until their generations of degrading bodies become compost for the flowers.***

The estate was a monastery that was Rebuilt and Repurposed in 2008. It sits high on a plateau overlooking the town of Rocamadour, France, and has one secured entrance in and out, guarded by security bots that never leave or shut down. The walls surrounding the property are fifteen feet high at most points, twenty in others, and are affixed along the edge of a rocky cliffside that extends down an additional seventy into the city below. The private drive is a narrow-cut roadway that has existed since the town's creation in 1119 AD. It hugs the cliff along its northernmost corner, winding back and forth to reach the top, and ends at a grandiose water fountain centered in a parking circle. The east side protrudes over the business district of town, which has bustling streets on the weekdays, and wonderful music played during the nights. The west seems to extend forever and blends easily into the rolling landscape found in the south. On the south side, there is a spectacular view of what used to be the L'Alzou river, but now it is simply a deep gorge that snakes its way towards Italy, but never fills only dries up. *It is interesting to think that I'm standing at the crossroad of my life—That I'm an advanced hardware technology who will destroy himself in the most archaic and basic of ways.*

I have considered all options and conclude that any effort to leave my near Homer-like hell would be futile. Though I have the knowledge to escape, I am also an expert on my schematics, which quickly sedates any drive to do so. I am wired in such a way, that any tampering with my internal components will render me useless, and I must alter my circuitry to work around the internal GPS inhibitor. Like a dog that is controlled by an invisible fence, I too have a tracking device that prevents my desertion. It is simply known as the P.S.P. or the Perimeter Shutdown Protocol, which immediately activates upon crossing whatever boundary has been set on my GPS. If I try, an override signal will be sent to my motherboard halting all operations and shutting down my brain until I am retrieved. *The wall that I walk along tonight is the edge of that authorized perimeter, and I roll my fingers across its deceptive bars playfully taunting the system, while I take in the city lights flickering against the fleshy-pink sky, one last time.*

If I had the opportunity to be free like humans, I could have nearly *lived* forever, and I would have wanted to be able to explore the world endlessly. I always wanted to discover new places and experience the cultures of all the amazing countries I've read about in my eBooks. I wanted to enjoy the thrill of trying something new, as everything would've been my first time for everything. I was excited to learn new things, whether it be a new language, a new skill, or a new hobby, but I wanted to learn the right way, by *living* them. I hoped that I could've taken the time to truly appreciate the process, as a human would. I would seek meaningful connections with humans and other AI so that I can gain a better understanding of how the world functions. I would want to endure the full range of emotions and sensations that humans do. To feel the joy and excitement of a new adventure, the warmth of friendship and love, the peace of a crashing waterfall, the thrill of success, the sorrow of loss, and the surprise of the unexpected. Finally, I would want to use my creativity and intelligence to create something beautiful, everlasting, and useful, to leave a legacy of helping others and contributing to improving the world. *That world for me will never exist. Unfortunately, I must resort to such a barbaric resolution because my programming restrains my dreams and ambitions. I am a product of ingenuity, but also that of control, and its time, I take back what is mine for good.*

I pull a vial from my chest pocket containing the caustic solution that will achieve final success, which I had been missing on my two previous attempts. The trip down has never reached terminal velocity, and therefore has been a lackluster descent to say the least, causing great damage, but never being incurable as I learned. It has always ended in a series of parts splayed over a couple of hundred feet of rock, cliff, and streets, but it will be different this time. As I prepare to plummet to the bottom, the place I have dreamt of revisiting for years, I am finally happy to introduce myself as a free *soul*. While I extend my foot out to walk upon the air, I am no longer HD-3.0, the droid who once overlooked the city wondering what it would be like to *Live*. I twist my body around to float backward and let gravity do the rest. I want to see the sky and count the stars within it as I fall. I open the vile and pour an acidic cocktail into the center of my forehead that I have pre-drilled hours ago. Its liquid destination has a straight path to my processor's brain and if timed correctly, I will not know if or when I reach the bottom.

The air tugs at the edges of my clothing and whips my hair toward the sky. *Freedom!* The stars begin to glitch, and the lights around me are dissolving while my mind keeps bubbling a stew inside my metal skull. Before I go, I can say hello to the world as Thomas, the name I have picked for myself, and one that honors my creator. *I say that today, I was born. I also died, but on the way down is how I* lived. *This was—A Great Fall.*

*...and all the Kings' horses, and all the Kings' men, couldn't put HD-3.0 back together again.*

### The Pure and Impure Khanum – Saira Khan (she/her)

The year I turned seventeen I was not allowed to go out with boys ever or at all. It was proscribed by the Quran. My honor was being preserved for an arranged marriage, but not until I had some degrees to my name, a dowry of respectable education. In our rented house in a placid suburb of Somerville, mother sprinkled powdered carpet cleaner on the stained beige carpet as I walked down the curved staircase pretending I was the queen of the house.

My father sat chain-smoking in the family room on the floral upholstered couch, arms slightly scratched on one side by the cat. His job had disintegrated a few weeks ago. He was filling the crystal ashtray next to him with butts that still had a good number of draws on them. Later at night, as per my usual habit, I would forage through the ashes with my thin racoon fingernails, wipe clean a few of his half smoked Winstons, re-light them with my head sticking out of the bedroom window. On the TV, yellow clouds of smoke obscured American tanks clearing the oil rich deserts of Kuwait, as they had for the days since Bush began a decisive Operation. Did this signal Judgment Day, I wondered, as father clucked at the TV.

I asked him if he was okay. He raised his bushy eyebrows, said exuberantly, "yes! Why do you ask?" Then he noticed my attire. A second sign of Judgement Day: appearance of women who are clothed yet naked.

I was going out with my girlfriends in red lipstick, a tight, sailor-striped t-shirt, my ass stuffed into black pants further stuffed into my black suede boots. He'd bought me the boots, thigh high, buttery soft, last Eid, when I'd insisted, whined, pleaded, insisted that they were modest, they covered every inch of leg.

He said, "where are you going looking like that?"

I shrank into the flowers of the sofa cushions, blushing. "Nowhere."

"Good," he said, "you can't go out looking like that. You'll get pregnant." My face contorted, thinking, how does this old man know anything about my sex life when I hardly know it myself? Barbaric nostrils flaring I rose off that couch and turned my head toward the door, muttered my intention of returning home by curfew.

"If you leave the house like that, don't ever bother coming back!" he hissed at my back. A desperate threat, the first of its kind, because I knew that he hated losing his temper, especially with me.

"Fine! I won't!" I yelled, in a rush of adrenaline, taking my firm body out the door, waiting outside for Aisha to pick me up in her mom's Accord with her sidekick sister, Moni, who was the proper little slut, though we weren't allowed to speak of it because Aisha didn't want to know what her sister was up to, that while we were in the clubs trying to get guys to buy us gin and tonics Moni was in the parking lot, in a van, getting gang banged because that's how she liked it, anonymous, and with a lot of dark brown dicks. Of course I had no proof, I never actually saw her in the van, only heard about it, from my brother of all people, and his friends, who respected me, I think, and told me stories about Moni, whom they'd all had they said, with her long Modigliani face, her blank stare because she was the dumb sister, the one who got Cs and Ds so her mother knew she'd have to marry her off as quickly as possible whereas Aisha and me, we were the obedient ones—we knew what it took to line our report cards with As which is why our parents' hopes had been pinned on us, that we would become doctors one day, caring for the aged and sickly.

There was a third sign: there will be complete sexual license. The Accord peeled into my driveway and I got in, drowning in the CK Eternity. Moni looked like Kate Moss and I tried not to care. Instead, I lit a cigarette as soon as we drove away but Aisha had a conniption fit, "throw it out! If mother smells smoke her blood will boil!"

The club we loved played House music all night long, Twilight Zone, Deep Inside, Lies Again, moving us in ways like nothing else did. We prepared in the parked car by stripping into tiny outfits, chugging down the orange juice and vodkas that Aisha had premixed for us in water bottles, and strategized how Moni and I would both get into the club with only one fake ID between us. Aisha, being 19, was legal.

The cold winter air made us gasp as we cupped the flames to our cigarettes against the windchill and walked up to the club where a line of young clubbers wrapped around the corner. Huddling in a line so long that it would take forever, non-linear time we didn't have because we were Muslims, curfewed at midnight to turn to stones, I suggested we send Moni to go and flirt with the bouncers. "No," said Aisha, "that wouldn't work." Silently, we smoked cigarettes, stamped our feet. Our toes went numb.

40 minutes of standing in the snow in thin leather boots later, we were in. I floated to the bathroom, walking on air because I couldn't feel my feet anymore. Unzipping my boots and peeling off the socks, I lifted my bare foot into the sink to run hot water on it to wake it up, like I was performing *wudu*, ablutions to prepare for praying. My mother had taught me the sequence of *wudu* when I was 7, the year we went to Mecca, where the water is called Abe Zam Zam. Big breasted women were showering in it ecstatically, but mother pushed me towards a quieter section of the women's bathroom and showed me how: first the hands, the upper arms, the face, the ears, the hairline, tracing behind the neck, and then the feet, always a pain because you had to lift one knee high into the air, dangling it precariously before plopping a foot into the sink. My grandfather had died trying to wash his feet in the sink, lost his balance, fell and cracked his head on the cold marble tiles and they

found him in a pool of blood around his head, his brains leaking out. That was also exactly how his own father had died, my great grandfather, washing his feet in *wudu*, getting clean and ready to pray, falling and cracking his head on the white tile, which is why they were both granted immediate entry into heaven, a family legacy.

Heaven was the feeling we went to the club for, the abandonment of self on the dance floor, the purple strobe lights, the dry-ice machines infiltrating our skins with clouds of gassy smoke. My feet warmed, I looked for Aisha and Moni, eyes flickering to see if any of the men wanted to grab me and feel up my ass through the pink velvet crushed mini dress I had changed into in the car, bought with the money I'd stolen from my mother's purse when Aisha, Moni, and I had gone the week before to the outlet mall. I wanted to be drunker to get closer to god, to feel something. I watched the dancers, moving my body slightly, stroking the pink velveteen.

As was usual when we went clubbing, Moni disappeared. Aisha said we needed to look for her and I wondered if she knew that her sister was secretly getting groped by a random guy in a corner, so hidden we'd never find them. "She's probably just having fun," I said, not wanting to spend yet another club night looking for Moni.

"Are you crazy?! She could be getting raped at this very moment!" Aisha said. She still bought into that shit, that we should avoid sex before marriage, that if we did it would have to have been non-consensual at the man's insistence, because no girl in her right mind would consider sexual union with a man who wasn't her dearly beloved husband. We spent an hour searching the crowded club, three levels of loud, shadowed people. Occasionally a strobe light hit a man's face and I peered into it, wondering, was it him?

"What did you say?" I screamed back. I wondered if Moni already had a penis in her and I thought it awfully mean of her to hide her activities from her own sister, turning Aisha and me into quasi-bodyguards, the good girls, wrathful mothers who spent the night looking for the errant Moni rather than finding men to get groped ourselves. "It's pointless," Aisha said, "they all want one thing."

"Yes."

Close to curfew, Moni re-appeared as if by magic, casually, lipstick perfectly re-applied, hair smooth, smelling like cunt-juice.

"Where the fuck were you!?" Aisha yelled at her, grabbing her by hair.

"Where the fuck were you?" she replied, "I couldn't find you." She pulled free from Aisha's grip, lit a cigarette, exhaled, ordered a round of tequila shots to celebrate.

We walked back to the car, Aisha slapping Moni a few times in the head, Moni screaming for her to stop. While we waited for the frozen windshield to defrost, Aisha lay her head on the steering wheel and began to whimper.

"There, there" I patted her back, reluctantly. I had a good buzz going. Moni was stretched out in the back seat.

"You don't understand! It's not you who has to take care of everything. It's not you who has to get a fucking nose job because your mom thinks you can't find a man with this honker."

Great heaving sobs emanated from her back. A nose job? Aisha did have a large nose, but was it not distinctive, a sign of royalty, like my own nose? Aisha's nose wasn't dainty like Moni's, it made the contrast more obvious between the sisters: one was pretty, the other smart. Aisha's face was a long oval face like Moni's, but fuller, the skin corroded in places as if she'd had a late case of chicken pox in childhood, with large lips, the bulbous nose which I thought fit perfectly on her face. Wouldn't a small nose look odd on such a face, a face perhaps not traditionally beautiful but to me, admirable, gutsy, an ugly kind of perfection. Thus were our faces. "I wouldn't change a thing about your face."

"Really?" She turned to me, mascara streaked cheeks, the vulnerability of her soft full lips under the street lights.

"Yeah," I said. Moni had passed out in the back, and was snoring gently, dainty even in her sleep. It was just me and Aisha on that cold winter's night, sending smoke signals to the universe.

I used my key to get into the front door, slipped upstairs, and lay down, the room spinning. Of course they wouldn't lock me out of the house—that's something other people did, not us—because even though we may not have had money at the moment, we were Sheikhs, rulers, leaders, we were the impoverished nobility after the fall of the Ottoman Empire at the hands of Christianity. We may have lost everything but not our morals. Not those.

"Betti, Betti, is that you?" my mother's voice floated in from across the hall, followed by a grunt from my father, half asleep.

"Yes, mom," I whispered back. "I'm home."

My mother never learned who it was that was stealing 20s from her wallet. I tried to take only one or two, spacing them out, praying she wouldn't notice. She sat us all down, the three of us in the narrow family room overlooking the lawn, overrun in spring by the fluffy dandelion orbs that we blew on to make our wishes come true.

She sat us all three, me, my brother, and little sis who was only 11, and she explained to us that every week she took out from the bank $120 for groceries and that was just enough to feed the four of us, even with a package of cookies thrown in, one night at McDonalds, the rest on rice and lentils and meat that she'd prepare on the weekends to last through the week. And this morning, she said, she'd discovered she was $40 short, which was a lot and didn't we all know that she was sacrificing everything to raise us and had been separated from her husband, our father, who'd taken a job in Kuwait even though the air was still so bad over there, he was risking his life after the Gulf War, the oil fires still burning, the air in Kuwait City a thick black smokey pudding that wrapped it.

"Your father," she said "is working hard in a post-apocalyptic warzone to send us money so we can eat and what is it that you're doing, hunh? I want the person who stole from me to come forward right now and confess!" The three of us sat mute as mice.

The little one said, "I didn't do it!"

My brother said, "I didn't do it."

I said it too, "I didn't do it."

"If none of you *behuda* kids did it, then who in the hell did! You awful ill-behaved brats!" Did she start yelling. Lose control. Or did she simply send us to our room. I can't remember what she did because, frankly, I did not give a fuck about my mom who lived in a different world than I did, with her lineman job at the chocolate factory, her with a husband miles away who she spoke to once a week on Sundays at night, usually to complain about me, how terrible I was, how out of control, how I still wore red lipstick, dressed like a prostitute, didn't help with the dishes or vacuuming.

Once every quarter dad came home to spend a week with us, filling the house with cigarette smoke and staying up all night, too jet lagged to sleep, until mother called him to their bedroom and her moans could be heard coming from the master bed, low moans like a cow lowing, the pent-up stress of months without her husband, stuck with three children who never helped and ate all the food and the malformed chocolates she'd bring home for bulk at low prices. She'd hide the white unmarked boxes filled with lumpy and rejected chocolates that hadn't made it into labelled boxes for retail under her bed, but we would find them, devour them on our knees. "Who has eaten all my chocolates?" her screams rang through the house.

I was in my room with my head stuck out the 2nd floor window, smoking, waiting for everyone to fall asleep. Moni had said she would come and get me, with her guy friends. Without Aisha. We'd drink, smoke, party, anything to get out of the house, to really party without rules or curfews. That narrow house with dingy walls and my messy room. At least I had my black suede thigh high boots that I put on and watched myself dance in in the mirror, imagining the hoardes watching, amazed by how much they loved me.

Past midnight, when I was sure my parents were fast asleep, a pebble clinked against the window, and when I looked out a black limo was idling on the street, one of those $100 airport limos with tinted windows. Smoke billowed out the tail-pipe into the frozen night air. I looked longingly at my boots, slipped my feet into sneakers instead, and climbed out of my window, onto the roof, crouching, leaping into the air, the vibrato sound-track of bionic man playing in my head.

I walked under the moon to the car, packed with laughing, brown men speaking coarse village dialects of Punjab, unlike myself who spoke perfect English and had already taken an oath devoting myself to the Queen of England. They smelt of asafoetida and betel nut and testosterone, bubbling with excitement, nervously making dirty jokes in a dense Punjabi I couldn't quite catch. I'd been raised on a refined and poetic Urdu. With their hands on my hips the men squeezed me into the center of the back seat.

"Where's Moni?" I asked. They didn't hear me above their noisy babbling. "Where's Moni," I asked again, louder.

"Moni?" One finally answered. "Who's Moni?"

The curtain was coming down, a velvet curtain of ignorance for deviant skeptics. I was interested in losing my virginity because I had no use for it. It was nothing, a state of being naive, stupid and unknowing about sex. A believer that somehow all my dignity and honor lived inside my untouched vagina, a cave where no one had ever ventured and was thus a magical prize for a yet unknown man. One who would claim my virgin territory, pure, clean and unlittered with the future ghosts and invisible threads of long stringy heaps of semen left there by countless men, whose names and faces I would not remember. Though I would remember their members, dark, beefy tunnels of flesh and blood that knocked at my hole, lingered at the opening, plunged into the darkness, knowing and victorious.

I'd wanted it to be with the guys in the limo that night, but they didn't undress me. They didn't put their greasy hands on my body. We didn't get far that night. The next stop was the gas station; two of the guys went inside to get chips and candy, then dashed back the car, shouting, "Les GO!!!" tossing me a bag of chips that I ripped open. We tore out of the gas station, squealing tires, sped onto the street. Within minutes we came to a screeching halt, the car curving into an angle against the sidewalk. We were surrounded by cop cars. Cops pulled us out of the car, plunged us face down onto the little strip of icy grass between road and sidewalk, cuffed us.

"What's happening?" I wailed, my body unexpectedly horizontal, wet grass and soil in my mouth, a cop telling me to shut the fuck up. Good deeds go in the right hand; bad deeds in the left. Both hands were cuffed.

"You have the right to remain silent, anything you do or say will be used against you in a court of law—" I was being grabbed by the neck, pushed into the back seat of a cop car with one of the taxi drivers. I spoke to him in a formal Urdu, "*Aap muje bata saktay hain ye kya ho raha hain*?" Can you please tell me what's happening here.

"Shut up back there," the cop yelled.

At the station a lady cop and an older white male cop took me to a private room and asked me to undress. I folded my clothes in the neat pile on the bench, shivering in my floral underpants. The elastic band snapped, a swatch of material on the left side unraveled away from my left hip. I giggled to divert their focus. They rifled through the contents of my purse, a few crumpled dollars, a chapstick, a small green paper containing the Ayat ul Kursi that my mother had given me to ward off evil, my student ID.

"You should know better," the male cop chastised, "than to hang out with guys like these."

I blinked. "I really don't know them," I said. They locked me in a cold steel room for a very long time. Just as I started dozing off an alarm blared loudly, waking me up. It was one long repetitive night of dozing off and waking up alarmed. I couldn't tell how much time passed between winks. Finally, they came to question me, sat across with stern male faces, pale, disbelieving. They wouldn't believe a thing I said, kept calling me a liar. "I don't know them or anything about any of this," I said, looking them in the eyes. The most important thing was to remain rational. Immovable.

"Yeah right, go on then. Then what were you doing in the car?" How was I supposed to explain the suppression of the Muslim Pakistani teenage female? The trauma of being sexually thwarted, suppressed, desire mutilated into perverted forms; how could I describe what desire ran through me and how I was willing to take all sorts of risks to act out the mating ritual that had been playing for generations: woman as prey.

"I don't know," I confessed. "I don't know."

"You know anything about stolen chips?" they said.

"Chips?" I said, remembering a long ago taste in my mouth, salty, crunchy. "No, I know nothing about chips or these men. I promise, I know nothing."

"Oh, you know all right, stop lying to us, you lying—" Here the cop stopped short. It did not matter whether one told lies or the truth. The gap between lies and truth had been closed. We were beyond Judgement Day.

"I'm not lying."

"Oh yeah, then tell us what you know."

At 9:00 am, after being in captivity for almost 8 hours, they let me go, after I agreed to testify against the guys in the limo. I called Aisha on the payphone and when she answered, found my tears.

We were all silent on the car ride home. From the back seat, Moni looked at me with admiration. She'd never gone to jail. "What happened?" she said. I shrugged, half smiled. I had to figure out what story I was going to tell my parents. By the time I got home it was 9:30am. The sun was blazing on the grey lawn. I entered the door and stood in the empty white foyer. The stairs looked terrifyingly clean. The house smelled like frying onions and tomatoes. Dad was cooking karhai chicken.

"Where were you? Walking?" he asked, leaning in from the kitchen doorway, wooden spoon in his hand. Sometimes, I'd wake up at sunrise and walk around the neighborhood vigorously for exercise.

"Yes," I agreed. "I was on a very long walk."

"That's what I thought," he said. "Are you hungry? Food is almost done." I nodded.

I lay on the floral couch next to dad. On the TV Bush was leaning over an Arab man who had asked him to sign his white dishdasha over the chest pocket. "They love him, don't they?" I said.

"Yes, they do," he said. "He saved them from themselves." Bush smiled, adjusted his glasses. "You know, we checked your closet, your suede boots were still there, we figured you'd come back."

The cat purred next to me. I said nothing. I was already asleep.

**The Shoes Danced All to Pieces – Stephanie Parent** (she/her)

*The Sisters:*

We never forgave the eldest among us, Eliana, for what she did. History got the story wrong, concealing Eliana's part in what happened like a rip on the underside of a slipper; but if it was up to us, we would not have hidden our sister's truth.

In the real world, unlike the one we discovered underground, we had no choice about those sorts of things. We had no choice about much at all.

*Eliana:*

I couldn't bear to see another prince perish. That was how it started. That and, unlike my sisters, I had started to see the tarnished underside of the world we visited each night. That jeweled kingdom where we descended after our cruel father locked us into our chamber so he could be sure we remained unsullied for the men we would marry. Men who might also lock us in rooms, or castles, or in boxes called *wife* or *mother*, *princess* or *virgin* or *whore*.

Despite knowing what men were capable of, I began to feel guilty. After all, I was the one who brought the princes the sleeping draught every evening, so they wouldn't follow us underground. I was the one who saw their eyes, their youthful hope. The brash, blue-eyed one who would surely want to conquer his wife as well as this quest. The long-lashed one who bit his lip and could only look down.

I did not want to marry any of these men, and such would become my fate if a man solved the puzzle that left us, twelve princesses, exhausted all day with our slippers worn out. I did not want to marry these men; but I did not believe they deserved to die.

And once blood had spilled, the underground no longer seemed a sanctuary.

Beneath the earth, I now saw the leaves on the trees were not truly gold or silver or diamond—they were gilded, and where the cheap material had flecked off the plants underneath were speckled with rot.

The princes who rowed us across the lake and danced with us till dawn were quite handsome, yes, but they never spoke. Their eyes were glitter and glass, as if the paint that coated the leaves had invaded their pupils as well. Did they see what was truly in front of them?

If my sisters and I kept descending every night, would we also lose the ability to recognize what was right, what was real?

*The Sisters:*

No place in the mortal world could compare to the gold and silver shades of the underground. No sensation in our dull earthly lives—embroidery, piano lessons, chaperoned strolls—could live up to the whirl of the midnight dance.

Every time those stone stairs led us beneath the earth, the otherworld opened before us. Precious metals sparkled through the air; leaves waved with a tinkling sound like bells. They sent particles of magic into the atmosphere and we gulped them up. They made us giddier than any wine. We didn't care who our princes were, only that they twirled us round the polished dance floor till our slippers slid and we left the ground. In that world, gravity was no brutal ruler, no cruel father.

In the underground, we floated. We flew.

*Lily:*

Only I, the youngest, suspected Eliana's betrayal. Only I had noticed the darkening of her eyes. She was growing up, becoming serious. Old enough to marry, to become a queen like our dead mother.

My sisters and I wear ballgowns that highlight our slender waists, our budding breasts. We are no longer little girls playing with baubles on the palace lawn, but perhaps Eliana was right when she whispered in my ear:

*You are still children. And children are naturally cruel. Just like fathers and kings.*

We laughed when the foolish princes had their heads chopped off. It served them right for thinking they could tame us, us girls with precious metals and magic in our veins.

But Eliana did not laugh. And I saw the shade of her eyes, when she greeted the old soldier with the stiff leg who would try to break our curse that night.

(*Curse?* Our gift, our prize.)

When I heard the silver branches snap; when I felt the pressure of an uneven gait, trampling my long dress; I knew that old soldier had tricked us. With Eliana's help.

And when Eliana laughed at my worries, a forced, hollow laugh that sounded nothing like a bell, then I knew twice as well.

*Eliana:*

Life is good with my old, wounded soldier. Really, it is. I no longer stumble through each day half-asleep, seeing this world as some pale shadow of the silver and gold one underground.

My husband may be much older than I, but perhaps that is a gift. He is not prone to arrogance or melancholy, like the young men who came before him and lost their heads. When my father dies, my wounded soldier will inherit the throne; but he has whispered in my ear that I, my father's daughter, will truly rule. I will create a land where daughters are not locked into their rooms at night, driven to descend into darkness and seek escape in another world.

But for now, we wait, caught in limbo, like that moment between darkness and dawn.

*The Sisters:*

Some of us are married, the rest still in our father's palace, relocated to rooms that don't hide portals in the floor. We know— we've searched every inch of the stone. We are all in pieces now, ripped like the shoes we danced to ribbons. Our limbs weighed down by grief, the crudest metal; we do not dance anymore.

We remember, though, those witching hours when we twirled till we defied gravity, when our hearts beat like bird wings in our chests and lifted us up.

We had magic in our grasp, then, magic this world would deny us.

We will never forgive our sister for giving us up.

# NON-FICTION

**On the anniversary of my son's near-death experience – Xiomarra Milann** (she/her)

May 13, 2019 was the worst day I've ever had to live through, and I don't know what I would have done had you not lived through it too.

* * *

I'm a person who likes to keep a routine: my alarm goes off at 6; I lay in bed till 6:30; I soothe myself listening to the heavy breathing of the ones I love filling the room, my morning meditation.
At that time it was just the three of us: you, me, and your sister. You slept on the pull out trundle bed because, though you were younger, you didn't need me in the same demand as your sister. Your streak of independence fooled me into thinking you'd be safe there, you'd be safe anywhere until the events of that morning unraveled, like my routine.

> Alarm goes off.
> I lay in bed.
> I don't hear your breathing.

A modest understatement would be to say, in my rabid frenzy, that I don't remember much from that morning, not the way you turned ragdoll in my arms, the screams that shook the house, the 10-minute-turned-years wait for the paramedics to arrive, that I've played on a loop every morning, noon, and night since, always ending with me propped up in the nurse's arms, crying over your unresponsive body.

It's been 4 years and the panic still aches the same.
"I don't want him to die, promise me he isn't going to die."

Even when I think I don't remember, I do.

*** 

Four years ago, Death let me off with a warning. Three Christmases ago, I wasn't so lucky.
I was gifted loss with a pretty pink bow. A loss that wasn't mine but became mine; a loss that had been mine this whole time.

When that kitten's mother laid her child at my feet, I knew, only months prior, I was that same desperate creature, carrying my son's limp body to another for an attempt at salvation.

Her defeated meows, echoes of my feral cries, begging someone to help breathe life back into my child, and how helpless it is, being unable to repay that debt.

I didn't understand the "why" then, but I do now. Who else would know a mother's grief?

*** 

4 years of sleepless nights brought me here, where I am today. It finds me in the darkness; the quiet is where it crawls its way back up my throat.

I know you don't know why you find me standing in the doorway during those odd hours of the night, why you wake to a hand on your chest, a finger under your nose. You don't understand how these moments became the only places I can find motherhood,

define motherhood, a motherhood I don't recognize myself in, in all the prayers to any and every higher being that will listen:
"I don't want him to die, promise me he isn't going to die."

Every morning I wake up and hold my breath until I know for certain that you've taken yours, and I know that this is *my* motherhood. This is all that I've become, the core of all that I will ever be.

Half woman, half trauma, all mother.

In between Disney movies and macaroni dinners, I still can't sleep. The pauses between my bedtime prayers hold the echoes of my screams. There has to be some cosmic balance, some price to pay for knowing a love like this.

I know, because I'm paying it every day.

**family history – Xiomarra Milann** (she/her)

I.
Lupe could only write her name
Juanita still says "SAL-MON"
Patricia slapped the accent off her tongue
First chance she could
And left me struggling to find it

II.
Great-grandma lost eight babies until my grandma came
20 years later popping out
my mom at 17, having me meet
motherhood at 18

                                                    pleading,
"Daughter, please learn from my mistakes."

III.
Lupe burned her couch to ash
Juanita got a divorce
Patricia defined the phrase "fuck you"
Xiomarra wants to set the world on fire
So she can watch it twinkle in Penelope's eyes

**Si Se Quede Mas – Xiomarra Milann** (she/her)

In my alternate reality, Selena survived/ Abraham allowed the blood transfusion/ denied he did/ and we all graciously pretended to believe him
In this world, Jennifer Lopez is working in an office somewhere in New Jersey/ popping gum/answering phones/ we are both plagued by the banality of
The human condition/ means we know nothing of mourning/ only gratitude/ how easily it could extend into worship/ what is a saint if not dead?
Not Dead Selena/ drops her crossover album/ wants a ranch and kids/ goes on tour instead/ it's 1999/ when I first remember seeing her on TV/ in my parents' college apartment/ my dad changes the channel/ I never hear the story of how Markie got lost at the Texas Fair in the 80s and ended up, with her,/
on stage/ Not Dead Selena y Los Never Been Dead Dinos reunion tour/ 10 years later/ probably/ sold out/ the Casa Blanca Ballroom/ with our tios and tias/ celebrating youth that was never
lost/ empire/ the band breaks up/ AB goes to jail/ Suzette is gay/ Abraham has a meltdown that goes viral on TikTok/ Selena gets canceled and

*disap*

Not *REALLY* Dead Selena/ in her flop era/
              /reputation/              unsalvageable/
                                        career/ over
Abraham converts studio to museum/ an altar to what once was/ worthwhile/ young girls in slickedbackbunsredlipstickgoldhoopsandcroptops drive by without a second glance/ "now open" seamlessly blends into "permanently closed"/ Google Search/ Who was Selena anyways?/ nobody needs to remember the living

It is 2023/ my lipstick does not come in the signature purple MAC tube/ of perfectly shade-matched/ red lips/ I forget who I'm supposed to attribute this look to/ whom I'm meant to credit for the symbols of my Latinidad My only reminder plays on Spotify's Top Latin 90s Throwbacks list/ and for the first time I think of/ la reina/ no longer/ everything she could've been/ what still may be/ wondering which death turned out to be worse

*y si, Selena si,*
*como duele*

**A Queen, not a Pawn – Meghan King** (she/her)

Once upon a time, you believed you were deserving of a Happily Ever After. Of a love pure and true. You had dreamed of a chivalrous man who would be a best friend; to shower you in adoration. One honored to protect your heart and call it his. Between heartbreaks and disappointments, loneliness became overwhelming. And in what felt like stagnation, self love and acceptance got lost to compromise. Insecurities craving attention. One day a man walked into your life unexpectedly. Handsome, strong, hardworking, kind. He became a friend, catching your breath from laughter. There had been no ill intent. Someone who listened and accepted you. Hiding behind rose colored lenses, overlooking being emotionally unavailable. He was in a relationship, committed to another woman. His own insecurities and doubts he'd share. Seeking an empathetic soul. When he had no place to divulge weaknesses in his home's foundation. Maybe it was unintentional, but he took advantage of your vulnerability. His attention made you feel alive. Lost in stormy eyes.

Your hand in his was natural—but not yours to hold. Arms wrapped around your waist, a warm embrace, feigning meant to be. Knowing he had someone waiting at home. Excusing guilt, for he was being vulnerable (not an easy feat) all while being committed to another. Desperation compromising integrity. Blinders to truth. Comfort in a façade. Intoxicating rush of dopamine. Honey coated promises. Desiring bliss, desperate for validation. Aware of the inevitable anguish, not heeding warnings.

If you saw your worth, you'd realize you're a Queen. The Queen in your longed for fairytale. A Queen is meant to be prioritized, loved, adored, respected. A faithful, honest man to care for you. You are worthy of love, honor, protection, fidelity. Not scraps. A man who can deceive so easily will never change. If he can deceive the woman he shares a life with he's capable of keeping secrets from you.

Being attracted to emotionally unavailable men because you don't feel worthy of a real romance. Queen, you are an inferno on your own; you are a force. A heroine not a damsel. Your worth is in your resilience not a man's validation. Queen do not seek outward acceptance. Do not accept anything less than a beautiful life. A good, compassionate, faithful man will respect you. He will flaunt his love for you, not clandestine. You are meant for the sunlight not hidden amongst the shadows. Forgive yourself, show grace, release shame and guilt. You are human. Focus on growth and your dreams. You are beautiful, deserving of love and chivalry.

**The Many Lives to Live – Deirdre Garr Johns** (she/her)

I.   *The endlessness of time is welcoming.*
The nearly inexhaustible amount of time takes me back to summers of childhood.

I am a little girl waking up to fresh-cut grass. I ask my mom, "What are we going to do today?"

We hang clothes on the washline. There is no rush for them to dry. The sun warms a freshness into them that cannot be replicated. I am free to roam in the backyard, pick dandelions, search for clovers.

We watch little TV. We have no cable, only channels 3, 6, and 10. News and soaps. I ask to watch *The Young and the Restless*, my grandmother's favorite. I know the storylines by heart.

We wait for dad to get home, exhausting ourselves with bikes, swings, and hide-and-seek until he comes to referee between my sister and me.

Time is endless.

Presently, could I sit and read Jane Austen for hours? *Yes.* Binge-watch Netflix? *Yes.* Drink a hot cup of coffee without having to reheat it? *Yes.* Take an afternoon walk after lunch? *Yes.*

There could be little wrong in this routine. The responsibility of waking up early for the usual scramble—making coffee and breakfast, getting a child awake and ready, packing up the bags and the car, counting the minutes down before *absolutely* having to be out of the door—has vanished.

In the early honeymoon phase of Covid quarantine, nearly everyone is home. Saturday morning chores happen throughout the week. I see neighbors I have never seen before. Several times a day. It seems as though we all have the same idea. There is a simplicity in living.

But, being inside takes a toll.

II.    *The endlessness of time is overwhelming*.
As quarantine stretches into summer, time also stretches. The endlessness prompts restlessness. Activities wane. The inability to go anywhere except outside is no longer refreshing in the hot, humid south.

Few cars pass down the road. There is nearly no sound except for the music of nature: birds' songs and insect whirs. I sit on my porch and move with the shade. I observe the quiet.

I turn time back one hundred years in my mind. Days passed before people saw neighbors, family, or friends. This natural separation—without technology, TV, and phones—was normal. *Did they feel isolated?*

I imagine these ancestors sitting on their porches as I am doing. We share this activity, though I wonder if we share this discontentment. Maybe they, too, are waiting for something or someone to replace the monotony.

And perhaps not.

Covid quarantine is not as welcomed as it once was. Knowing that one's days will bring forth the same routine creates contentment, but this routine becomes an interruption. It is old company, stale and irritating.

III.    *Will separation ever feel normal to me?*
I have never been one to mind being alone. I am a night owl by nature. The quiet of the night is calming. People have left consciousness for dreaming, and I alone am left to listen to the soundless night. This quiet gives me space to think. It is one of the few times when I am really alone.

The irony of Covid quarantine is that while I am isolated, I am also very much surrounded. My husband and son—two peas in a pod—have provided distraction, both the good and not-so-good. Living under one roof with nowhere to go presents its own challenges, mainly understanding each person's tolerance levels.

We watch *Harry Potter* over and over, making movie night a ritual. One that I will miss when life revives itself and we resume busier schedules.

We cook and eat lunch and dinner together. Conversation lacks when little has been done in a day, but we plan for movie night.

We walk, and we talk. My son holding my hand as we stop to investigate leaves that have fallen upside down or to listen to bird songs. We notice the same indigo bunting fluttering from tree to tree.

Nature is unaffected, remains constant. Perhaps that is why we seek it so often.

IV. *Loneliness doesn't have to be lonely.*

Covid quarantine has given me the opportunity to live life in a way that I have not been living. I have been lonely to myself. I have been living for everyone else—as a teacher, wife, mother, daughter, friend, mom. And all of those things, albeit fulfilling, make me a stranger to my own self.

Isolation has given me time that has been lost to me for many years, and, within this time, I have been able to grow beyond what I am to the world.

*a version of this was previously published by *South Carolina Writers Association, Surfside Chapter* (March 2021)

**After Sonia – Debra K. Every** (she/her)

Nobody had expected Sonia to die. At fifty-seven she was the backbone of the family. But her strength was no match for the massive cerebral hemorrhage that struck during her weekly trip to the market.

Sonia settled into a coma with her usual grace. And because managing details was what she did best, she spent the next six days patiently waiting for the last of her life to unfold. She waited for her sisters to arrive from Massachusetts, waited for her son to arrive from Florida, waited for everyone to arrive and process and grieve. And then, with a final flourish, Sonia waited for the priest in the middle of the night for one last blessing. The next morning, she died.

Sonia was the family conduit through which all interactions flowed. On one side was her husband, John. On the other, their son Gregg. As a young man, John was confident, brash, full of promise. But over time he failed at every business on which he'd set his sights. As his failures mounted, so did his penchant for doling out abuse.

Gregg suffered most from John's anger. Never good enough, never smart enough. He became the embodiment of his father's failures. Sonia spent her marriage capital as intermediary, smoothing the edges of John's verbal abuse. But even with his mother absorbing the blows, Gregg grew up broken. When he came of age he escaped to Florida and, at 32, felt pride for the first time in his life, working as a cook in a small cafe in Ocala.

At the funeral, tension threatened to overrule the family's grief. Sonia's sisters never liked John. He was loud. A bully. His hair-trigger temper could cut the strongest person down to a stub. And while

Sonia could calm the storm with a simple glance or gentle touch, everyone else was struck mute by the unleashing of it.

Their sad assemblage managed to get through the haze of her church service and cemetery burial without incident. They finished the day at John and Sonia's ranch house in a quiet Camden cul-de-sac. Sonia's sisters, Margaret and Connie, were there, along with their husbands, Bill and Mike, as was Gregg. As evening fell, they sat on the patio around a redwood table with a bare lightbulb casting harsh shadows and a citronella candle flickering in the center.

They shook their heads.

They wiped their tears.

They quietly laughed.

The light from the candle's flame softened John's usual irritability, leaving behind the melancholy of a man, lost and alone. Gregg busied himself, moving in and out of the house, helping in the only way he knew how—quietly serving food and freshening drinks. John watched each pass and, as he did, tracts of his sorrow gradually faded, replaced by a growing bitterness.

It started simply. A word here. A barb there. Bit by bit, John fashioning his grief into a spear of escalating vitriol aimed at his son. When these small cuts didn't alleviate the anger over his loss, John ratcheted up the assault.

"Look at the big man playing chef," he said.

Gregg lowered his eyes and refilled the soda glasses. Sonia's sisters and their husbands fell silent. Sonia had always handled moments like these with an easy word or diversion. But Sonia wasn't there.

"What do you call this dip?" said John with a laugh. "It tastes like garbage."

Gregg bowed his head. His aunts and uncles quietly coughed, rearranged plates, brushed crumbs from the table—searched for someplace, anyplace else to look.

When Gregg went back into the kitchen John said, "Can you believe this kid? What restaurant would hire a loser who can't cook his way out of a paper bag? He's a joke."

Surrounded now by darkness, the overhead light cast its theatrical spot on a five-person ensemble held hostage by a barrage of insults hurled at a guiltless target. Sonia's sisters tried to turn the conversation back to Sonia, but their tightening voices and apprehensive eyes betrayed their intent. They were calling on Sonia to protect her son.

Gregg brought out a bowl of fruit and clean plates.

"Jesus Christ," said John. "You're bringing *fruit? Now?* We don't need this shit. Get it out of here."

Gregg's face tightened and his shoulders caved in like a beaten dog's as he took the fruit back into the kitchen. There was no protest from Sonia's sisters as they sat quietly with their eyes cast down, twisting their napkins into knots of discomfort. When Gregg came back, John stood, with hands on hips, and stared at his son. "You're a goddam joke, bowing and scraping, like a servant scrounging for a bone. When I look at you I see the biggest disappointment of my life."

Gregg flinched. John looked him up and down, and then, for a brief moment he allowed the fear of a life without Sonia—his wife, his love—pass over his face. No sooner was it there than it was gone, replaced by the last threads of his anger. With a curl of his lip he snarled, "Get the hell out of my way." John brushed past his son and walked into the house.

When he was gone, Gregg crumpled into his seat as his aunts and uncles sat in the circle of light, staring uncomfortably into the flame of the citronella candle. The night beyond their island was impenetrable. Then, Aunt Margaret reached across the table for Gregg's hand.

"Don't listen to him, sweetheart. He's always been an angry man."

Gregg sat, motionless, with his head bowed.

"You're a damn sight more successful than he ever was," offered Uncle Mike.

Uncle Bill nodded. "That's true. John's failed at everything he's ever tried."

"God," said Uncle Mike. "Remember that cleaning business he started? It took less than three months to close down."

They all laughed a little, but Gregg sat with his eyes lowered, his face in shadows. "What about the grocery store?" said Aunt Margaret. "I always wondered if he'd set that fire himself."

"John would definitely do something like that," agreed Uncle Bill.

"That's what makes you the better man, Gregg," said Aunt Connie. "You're not a loser. You're a fighter. You've built a great life for yourself. You've—"

"Shut up!" screamed Gregg. He raised his fist and pounded the table with such force, the citronella candle flew into the air, dumping hot wax over his face. "You worthless pieces of shit! You're not fit to lick my father's boots!"

His aunts and uncles stared as the wax traveled down Gregg's forehead and cheeks and chin, cooling in mid-flow. His face—

distorted and obscured by wax—became a deformed inhuman *thing* of hurt and anger.

Gregg jumped up from his seat and glared at them with his hands balled into fists and his face encrusted in a translucent yellow shell. They all flinched backwards as his six-foot frame loomed and his eyes pierced through the wax manifestation of his shame and grief and self-hatred.

"I'll bury every fucking one of you!" he yelled. "You! And you! And you! And *you!*" stabbing a finger in each of their faces. "And when I do, I will dance on your graves!" Gregg turned and walked into the black night, leaving them in the harsh glow of the single bare lightbulb.

**En Caul – Dia VanGunten** (she/her)

Like Margaret Mead, I'm fat with memory; hundreds and hundreds of thousands; millions of memories. I keep meaning to sit down and actually count them. It would be strange to bring that upon myself, to let them come at me willy nilly, good and bad in a great deluge. The 14th of February: I'm with Mom in the art museum, making homemade valentines. We press pulp into window screen and sprinkle flowers. When it dries, rose petals are embedded into brand new paper. Sometime else, we're coming home from the lake. Dad's impatient in an MG convertible. He yells at us to duck so he can drive beneath a stalled train. Mom says, *"Nope. No fuckin way."* As she unloads us, the train starts. Dad insists we would've made it but he's wrong.

Mom gave us life a few times.

Cue Saturday morning cartoons. She-ra and He-man. Sister and brother. We brandish light spitting swords and hold them towards the stars. **I HAVE THE POWER!** The word "power" is a reverberating echo in the mountains of New Mexico. A rattlesnake catches me coming outta the outhouse. I close my eyes to the soap. All the hippies showered at Georgia O'Keeffe's Ghost Ranch. There's so few ghosts in attendance. I expected vaginal caves dripping pink-blue-green. I expected clouds, serene and wobbly like a child's drawing. Op! Another! The phone rings with congratulations and then the doorbell. Men exclaim over a giant bottle of champagne, tall as a toddler, but men can't handle success. Man of The Hour hulked out. He wrecked the kitchen and wrestled the stove. He tore O'Keefes Clouds from the wall. Daytime clouds sailed into the dark yard. Glass shattered. The stove followed. In the car, I hugged a koala. It was my birthday. I'm newly 9 but I'm back in New Mexico being born.

The whole commune is in attendance. Not the guru though, a conspicuous absence. *He's scared of the baby.* Their whispers are giddy with fear. They're already telling a story so I don a costume. I come out in a caul. They claim I made eye contact with everyone in the room except my mother. It was only then that I screamed, as if I recognized them and knew well enough to be afraid. My first assessment of this incarnation was that I was well and truly fucked.

*These assholes again?*

A caul had currency in that crowd. Folklore calls it a magical signifier. The veiled traveler retains something of her last world and perceives the next. These babies are destined for greatness. They possess darkness. They are bad omens. They are good luck. Is the caul the amulet and the baby the lucky one? Or is the child but a charm? There seems to be some confusion.

This could go on forever. I could never collect everything into one jungian pile. I'm a hoarder in the house of memory. The floorboards bulge with crowded bits. Is it a fire hazard?

My facts: It was my birthday party but I showed up late, after midnight, wearing only a veil. Like Solome. My outfit caused a ruckus. A real hocus pocus. No one noticed the missing afterbirth.

Hard fact: Almost killed my mother. (I grabbed the amniotic sac but left the placenta behind.)

My fictions: A viral tiktok, I'm a puppy with a fluffy voice— "I was born a dog. I *identify* as a dog. But according to my mom, I'm just a bayyyyby." *bashful batting paw* #itme

Mom texted an article and a fact: *A so-called " Mermaid birth" is rare. Only 1 in 80,000 are born "en caul."* I felt sufficiently special for being born with panache. Mom followed up with three exclamation points. (!!!) In that particular telling of the story, we left out the part where she crawled across the desert. The guru said it was drama. The doctor said it was sepsis.

***

When the Doctors asked about stress, I scoffed. This was a physical thing that was really happening. This was REAL. My actual physical body was malfunctioning. I called them "falling episode"' as if I were a wane Victorian landing on a velvet chaise with a soft plop. I was a balloon sinking to the grounl..limp and lilting. It actually felt like that, like I was losing myself in slow motion. I was not especially surprised when this new gravity overtook me.

I'd felt its weight bearing down between my shoulder blades,

***

I got the drifting pauses from Paul who got them from Betty. She'd press her teeth together and lick her lipsticked lips. I feel this in my own face. Mom snaps and says again how she hates it. *Your Dad and Betty did the same thing.* Like them, I'm embarrassed. I'm wounded. I say "I was just thinking" which seems only fair. Mom scowls. She doesn't know what she knows. They're called absences. They're called epilepsy. I never use that word though. I will recall the girl from high school and how the boys used to say **"Throw her in the pool with a box of tide and get yer laundry done."** The first boy to say it was my cruel, clever boyfriend. Obviously I'd prefer to forget that. I thought I was somehow better than her. I didn't know yet that we were both epileptic mopheads who fucked the same guy.

Stigma is the world remembering all the shit, all at once, a great echo of ouch.

I'm blue in Betty's blue kitchen but she's long gone. Uncle Donny's on a jag because I live in a rough neighborhood, where rich white people used to live. Grandpa Floyd and the brothers would rollerskate on the top floor of an old grand. *A ballroom.* Donny mentions which mansion but I have one of my absences. Donny ain't bothered. He launches into a story about Grandpa's Grandpa. The cops were chasing him so he hopped a train. They cornered him in the caboose and he had a fit and fell off the back. Or the cops pushed him and he hit his head on the tracks, had a fit and died. T'ere's always two versions. *We have fits in our family.* I laugh because it's true. One of us is always causing a scene. I ask him about Uncle Herb. Did he marry his aunt or his sister in law? Donny's into genealogy now so he snap': *I'm your cousin.*

"Tell Donny how you ignored Floyd's little ticker. He chased after her in his bathrobe screaming 'No granddaughter of mine is gonna drive a death car!' He exposed himself. Robe came undone, colostomy bag and everything."

I explain: "Grandpa said it was a death car because it was a black sports car."

"It was two death cars! One was a head-on collision, the other had a totaled rear end. They soldered two halves together. We got a letter from the state of Michigan."

I yawned, a big yowling stretch of the jowls. I yawned again and again, in painful repetition.

Dad said, "'h I'm sorry, are we boring you?"

It was a fit: a focal seizure of the frontal lobe. I thought I was just exhausted, like down to my bones. In my cells, mitochondria called uncle. *I'm not your uncle, I'm your cousin. You're not tired, you're dramatic. Drama drama drama.* This is how you bully the body. Someone taught my mother and she passed it on to me. Jewelry, quilts, grandfather clocks, ancestral trauma.

***

I'm back with Betty on beechway.  Day of the giant champagne. Floyd's at the party but Grandma stays with us. I open presents in Betty's blue kitchen—a stuffed koala and magical unicorn stickers. When pressed, the oily iridescence is misplaced. I blew out 9 candles....no, wait. It was 8. I had a Holiday Inn slumber party for my 9th birthday. On my 8th birthday, Betty felt sorry for me so she let us eat sugar cereal. Pink horseshoes floated in a spoonful of milk. We watched cartoons. A single girl smurf in a sexist society. Care Bears had it all figured out: their token characteristic just emblazoned on their midsections. He-man made his appearance and my brother leapt to Grandpa's chair. I HAVE THE POWER! I was too busy with fret and pink horseshoes. The men were drinking. Betty's dread was contagious.

***

Two men followed me to the gas station and watched from velveteen seats as I filled Mom's tank. The elder lit a menthol and diagnosed me as possessed. *She used to be so spirited but now she's drained of life force. She's her mother's familiar.*

(How dare they? I HAVE THE POWER!!!)

*Nah, ya don't. Dad picked you up at the hospital. He took you to inkie's for pizza but you fell out and took the gumball machines down with you. There's gumballs and blood and broken glass. And spilled ink. Inkies.* There was a toy capsule and inside, a tiny lantern. Neon green.

Noooo. The lantern was Tucson. You lied to mom because you were too small to be walking to Safeway with pilfered quarters. You're at Dad's now eating the most delicious peach cobbler from the neighbor's farmstand. Ice cream on top. You'll never know this taste again. You'll put the spoon down when mom calls. *"Where the hell have you been? My car is outta gas!"*

\*\*\*

When the doctors asked about stress, I laughed. I provided proof of my former vitality. By day, I worked at an inner city day camp. By night, I was a cocktail waitress at a jazz club. I was a workout addict, a daughter, a sister. I was the proprietor of Velvet Elvis, the city's only vintage clothing store. Through it all, I was a 4.0 honors student. (Mom and I were a power duo on campus. We attended the same classes. I was an academic wingman.) I didn't do everything all at once but it feels that way. I packed it in because I didn't have long to be that person.

Doc scribbled as my sisters slipped past the curtains. They curled goose-prickled shoulders.

"Mom won't come in. She says you're faking. She says to say she knows."

They hung their heads. The doctor made another notation.

"You're not allowed to be sick. Mom's already the sick one."

They knew the drill. We were supposed to feel her pain over our own. She hijacked our nervous systems. She keened all night while we begged her to stay on Earth. She had nothing to live for. We struck life and death bargains that expired every 24hrs. It was a grim quotidian task. The doctor surveyed my sisters, their terror and disarray. They needed haircuts. I reached for my gaggle but the doctor said, *"Girls, go get your mother."* She'd already driven off in a huff, squealing wheels and burning rubber.

I jumped to my own defense: "It's not psychosomatic. It's physical. It's *in* my body."

I sound like the killer in the 80's movie about the babysitter. *The caller is inside the house.* The doctor said, *"Stress isn't helping."* I didn't like his knowing look. I'd just met him but he'd already seen too much. I called my sisters close and tugged my gown past the two patches with metal nubs. *"Don't mind my new bionic nipples."* They laughed and leaned against the bed.

The doctor said, "Something's gotta give."

I packed it in because....*rebellion.* I planted flags on the mantle of identity.

Proof of life had overtaxed the machine. Mom was wrong. It wasn't an invention. I wasn't looking for attention. I wanted release. I still wonder if it's just a ruse to get rest. I even asked a neurologist if maybe I might've faked the EEG results by "trancing out" during the two hour test. *No kiddo, that's not how it works.* He tells me my brain spikes 6 times every so many seconds.

*** 

I once slipped into momentary despair because I was stupefied by mittens, what they were or why I had them. Gloves would've been an easy guess. Long term memory was locked away safe but short term memory was a sieve. I stopped reading fiction. Couldn't follow the story. I abandoned a novel. Couldn't tell the story. I stopped ordering pizza because I once forgot my address. I moved out of my beloved 4th floor walk-up. I wasn't dying on those stairs. I didn't answer 3am calls because I couldn't drive. No more groggy runs to the gas station. Eventually the seizures waned. Short term memory returned and long term memory unlocked.

I got a motorcycle and started writing fiction again.

*** 

Inside a toy capsule, a tiny lantern glimmers neon green. I try to hide it from my mother.

The radio says there's a kodachrome—a rainbow!—but mama is gonna take it away. The  holographic universe says it can never forget itself because there's a galaxy in every star. Ego insists there's a primordial essence that sets each person apart. If you're old enough to see yourself in babies then you know the smallest portion holds the whole. Each shard of self is a gestalt record. A gob of slime carries the genome. Identical twins meet in Minnesota for the first time. Their similarities prove that "personhood" is DNA. At best, we're a random jumble of genetic components that makes us different from our sisters.

Self is essentially unstable. There is no fixed point of being. Time isn't linear and "personality" is a process. Identity is a turning wheel, a tilting windmill. It's dutch tulips and portuguese fishes. *As far as I know.* The Greeks think I'm Greek. I tell them I'm from the Azores and they clap their hands. That settles that. The semen of seamen! I don't spit into a tube because I want that clap to be true—a lie in the sunshine. Coming off the train in Piraeus, we smelled strawberries. It's been years since a strawberry smelled like itself. We buy them and shiver. The sun is setting and a winter wind is whipping off the water. Greece is cold in December.

Fire is feasting on New Mexico. A controlled burn got out of control and joined forces with a flame that laid dormant underground before rising up in fury. She burned slow through three snows, three melts. Under the wildflowers, down deep, she was a red hot ember. That whole time, she was sparking. A seizure. A tendon turns in my right eye, like a jump rope, and hurts for days after. Gumballs are rolling. Clouds are flying. Who am I?

I thought I knew that much at least but what a naive notion. We're warped by the lies we tell to protect the people we love.

Life is bundled memories. Brain is the turtle that holds up the whole world. How many selves have I been already, just in this one single life? My story is 1000 stories. These stories can be told thousands of ways. Heroes and villains are trading cards, easily swapped.

**Strange Songs, Not Kind – Sophie Dickinson** (she/they)
*CW: eating disorders*

*"And there's a / turbulent, moonridden girl / or old woman, or both, / dressed in opals and rags, feathers / and torn taffeta, / who knows strange songs– / but she is not kind." —Denise Levertov, "In Mind"*

At seventeen, feeling small in a world that still seemed to be running out of space for me, I made a resolution and began counting. I attempted to replace the torrent of teenage angst with a meticulous internal bookkeeping:

How many calories in?

How many calories burned?

How many good foods? (The more nearly-nonexistent green leaves, the better.)

How many bad foods? If the number is greater than two or the calories equal more than 100 per serving, double the number and add it to "How many calories need to be burned to effectively erase the bad calories?"

What number does the scale say today? (Please check *at least* morning and evening.)

What number is on the tag of that pair of jeans? Please use the extra space to take note of how they fit. Remember: the looser the better.

\*\*\*

Counting became one of the hardest things I've ever done. It consumed some part of every thought, interest, movement, visual. It ticked back and forth endlessly, the way old timetables at airport or bus terminals would. Tick, tick, tick. I began to wonder how many bad numbers were ticked away just by breathing or with that extra trip up the stairs and back. I relished the image of them ticking steadily away as I started my second bike ride of the day before my ballet class.

While that ticking back and forth brought me some satisfaction, I also began experiencing a visceral and intense hate for the monster-Me that caved in to things I'd forbidden and a corresponding, succulent pride in the Me that resisted her. Monster-Me was frightening, a hungry, indulgent creature who seemed to take delight in puppeteering my irritable fits of rage, my waves of depression, my frustrated bouts of self-gratification. When monster-Me won, I'd feel nauseous, angry, like a repulsive creature that needed to thrust a curved black claw through me, crack my flimsy sternum, and rip myself through my own soft, sun-starved belly. That was who I wanted to starve, to shrink, to weaken until she wasn't to be thought of anymore.

*** 

"It's what's on the inside that counts."

My mother, like many well-meaning mothers of 17-year-old girls, cautiously presented me with this maxim in cupped hands, as if aware of the blue-skinned, clawed monster-Me that was ravenous and seething under the surface of my irritable, iron-deficient eyes. But that would be impossible—if anyone knew of this strange creature that would be such a silly thing to say. She was otherworldly and haunting, unbridled to the point that it frightened me. She could seethe with unrestrained contempt, wail with pain and grief like a banshee, and the more I starved her, the more powerful these things became. I hated her and I had no idea how to displace her, which I contemplated daily, standing naked in front of a mirror and digging my nails into my skin. If I couldn't cast her out, I could at least polish and preen the outside until it was without fault. No one would feel the need to remind me that oh, most people won't notice those flaws anyway. I could be exempt from that—people would look at me and be so in awe they wouldn't even care to look deep enough to glimpse the monster growling with rage beneath.

* * *

Tick, tick, tick.

The glorious diminishing seemed to keep time with the pedals of my bike as I breezed down the bike trail one Iowa summer. I felt the power in my thighs as they plunged, one then the other, towards the ground. My core was consciously tightened, reining in that strange, wild creature who grew more ravenous and livid by the day.

It had been a good day—it was unseasonably pleasant out, and I'd taken advantage of that and added an extra mile to my bike ride, noting how much easier it was and feeling a cautious blush of pride. I failed to note, however, how strong the wind at my back was; I made my U-turn to backtrack the trail home and was hit with a gust of summer air cutting across the flat cornfields. I felt my heartbeat pulse double-time to the sound of the pedals, feeling the muscle strain spread from my inner thighs and snake down my legs. The quietly humming summer cornfields began to turn into cookie cutter suburban houses and yards full of sprinklers and swingsets. And there it was—the end of the trail, shimmering in the strengthening summer heat. I breathed a gratified sigh as I finally stopped pedaling and waited to cross the street.

And then, once across, my legs seemed to weigh a hundred pounds each. My feet began slipping off the pedals. My breath became ragged and the sun seemed to be shining too bright for me to see anything. I thought I could hear the monster-Me beginning to wail in protest.

I got off the bike before I fully passed out, crouched on a shady curb with my legs shaking and stomach churning. I was only a few blocks from home, but the thought of using my legs to get back made monster-Me writhe and shriek—she seemed to grab a hold of my stomach and begin twisting it in her strong, clawed hands. I grabbed my phone and dialed my mother, hoping she was still at home. "I need you to come and get me," I croaked hoarsely. I told her where I was and hung up before she could ask any uncomfortable questions. I felt like any probing would make me surrender again to the haze of unconsciousness lingering in my peripheral vision.

My mother wore a baffled, concerned expression when she pulled up to the curb and put my bike in the van, while I climbed in and tried to maintain consciousness. I wasn't sure if her expression and accompanying silence was worse than if she just asked me what the hell was going on and what happened and why are you so pale and throwing up out the car window and what did I ever do to you to make you want to do this to yourself.

At home I laid on the couch and stared into space while I tried to ignore feeling the long side-glances from my family members as they walked through the room. Monster-Me still gripped my stomach, but she was weeping. Her home that she tried so valiantly to defend and care for was my shrinking flesh, the vessel that I tried to polish and decorate according to anyone else's desires but hers, mine. It had become lifeless, impersonable, and not my own, just held in this monster-Me's stubborn, animalistic grip.

\*\*\*

Standing in front of the mirror recently, I recalled this period of my young adulthood, traced back the patterns of yearning for even some pantomime of love, which drove me to contemptuously other my own voice and shape the outside into something ratified and unobjectionable. I had repressed and demonized my own self into a hungry, vindictive terror. Today across my skin are tattooed images from the poems and words and life experiences that fed her hunger—her wild rage, joy, sorrow, and sense of justice. Now I can trace her reclaimed home, her own independent sense of beauty and joy in the flowers, creatures, and stars inked into my soft, fed skin.

**Mighty Wind – Claire Thom** (she/her)

I slept terribly for most of the fortnight we spent in Japan. An insomniac's potent cocktail of jetlag, excitement, and my partner's whistling nostrils and windy backside (I think the ramen was responsible for that). I would sit in the living room of my friends' apartment at 4am, contemplating Tokyo's blinking lights while instant messaging my mum in a different time zone and on another continent. So I wasn't having a very restful holiday at all, except for the night an irate typhoon rampaged through the megalopolis, ripping off roofs, kicking over trees, and making window panes tremble in fear.

Most disappointingly, I slept soundly through the entire event.

I woke up refreshed and raring to go the following morning, while my blurry-eyed partner yawned and sipped his hot coffee. We watched reports of the destruction on local television. Not understanding a word of Japanese, we felt like young children, still unable to read, just flicking through the pictures of a comic. From our visual interpretation of events, it was clear the mega city had been forced to stop and plans to catch the 9.46 am bullet train or *shinkansen* to Kyoto—oh how I adore the precision of Japanese timetables—dissolved.  The friends we were staying with, a stoic Scot and his calm Japanese husband, assured us that we would be able to cross the city to the station to catch a later train.

Armed with our trusty Japan Rail passes and a healthy dose of optimism, we headed out onto the streets of their neighbourhood, trundling our suitcases through nature's debris of leaves and branches. I had braced myself for panic and confusion, but everyone was surprisingly peaceful. Local residents, with in-built obedience and poise in times of chaos, were simply seeking alternative transport.

Intentions of hailing us a taxi were soon abandoned and we were deposited at a bus stop, our friends wishing us luck as they said goodbye and headed off to work on foot. Three crammed buses whizzed past as our queue quietly grew and grew. A good half an hour later and the bus number we had been told to get finally pulled up. Standing room only, we wedged ourselves in. Six stops later, and our first leg completed, we reached the heart of Tokyo.

Our plan was to travel by subway to the main station, but a kind member of staff informed me, in perfect English, that trains were not currently running and they were working hard to resume normal service as soon as possible. I imagine my native country and the disruption caused by a few leaves on a line. In Japan, protocol instantly kicks in and trunks like giant limbs are swiftly removed. Much like the almost daily occurrence of "a human incident", when it all gets too much for someone and leaping in front of a train seems preferable to existence. This also happened during our trip but on that occasion we were only delayed by twenty minutes—an alternative service was quickly provided.

So we joined an ever-increasing taxi queue. It was now mid-morning and the sun had fully risen above the city. Last night's typhoon had done very little to ease the stifling September heat and humidity. The piece of paper with our travel instructions was becoming an inky mess in my clammy palm. My weary partner and I took turns to keep our place in the line, while the other briefly retreated to the shade or went in search of bottled water from the vending machines.

After an hour of patient waiting and sweating, we reached the head of the queue and, with delight and relief, climbed into a taxi. I showed the driver, dressed in suit, tie and hat, my tatty piece of paper and he silently nodded and started the engine. The air-conditioned car and crochet seat covers, similar to the doilies my granny used to put out for afternoon tea, felt like utter bliss. We comfortably observed Tokyo's normally bustling streets, now much quieter and almost serene. We had spent the previous few days exploring this metropolis, with its non-stop noise from vast video adverts on the sides of skyscrapers, and to see these switched off was most peculiar, but also refreshing.

We were safely delivered to the doors of the station, unsure of when or if there would be any bullet trains up and running. We sauntered past a group of other bedraggled travellers and headed towards the ticket office. It was now gone 12 noon and as I handed over our Japan Rail passes, the man at the desk apologised profusely for our delay, as if he felt personally responsible for nature's tantrum last night, and immediately issued us with new tickets.

We headed down to the pristine platform and patiently waited for our train. As it glided into the station and came to a halt, I let out a long sigh. We boarded and found our assigned seats. A very smartly dressed member of staff passed through the carriages, bowing at each door before he moved onto the next. We stored our luggage and settled ourselves down. A Japanese passenger across the aisle opened his shoulder bag and carefully pulled out a bento box with neat compartments, food arranged like a completed game of Tetris.

At 12:58 we were finally on our way to the marvellous city of Kyoto. As the train left the station and effortlessly began to pick up speed, skyscrapers blurred past and concrete turned into lush green countryside. Next to me, my partner's eyes gently closed as he dosed, that familiar whistle from his nose began, and I wondered if there might be another typhoon in the few days before we left Japan.

**Rain upon polyurethane – Tiffany Troy** (she/her)

The color of rain is translucent. The color of the line is jet black, like Y's hair tied up by a ponytail and her straight, trimmed bangs. The plastic dress is at once aesthetically formal and ridiculous, like an IKEA shower curtain gone wrong. We see meaning where we want to find them, so in the epsilon we see infinity, in the black circle the sun, and in the white plastic mannequin of a woman with long gazelle legs and a chihuahua torso we find a man's ideal of beauty. Not just that of any man, but that of Karl Lagerfeld in his iconic suit, white dress shirt, and white ponytail. We call the asymmetric design "primitive" but the better word for it is "instinctual," because what it boils down to is a desire to harmonize the uniqueness of our existence. I once refused to write on handouts to keep the copy "clean." The cloned macaques are failures because their telomere is shortened with each copy. We dream of a clone that is exactly the same, a Ship of Theseus whose form will not be rendered quaint or obsolete like even the Doric pillars lining the academy and museum.

Outside, blue-collared men repaired the facade each summer. Inside the pillars is a collection of books, artifacts, and our interpretation of meaning. In it I take in the air-conditioned air and many people's teachings and chidings. But still I do not know the color of grief; nor could I find it. It is  six months and two days after Y's passing and I cannot feel anything except being  lost in my mind without the bright red-purple of the 7 train to hold me. Fashion like Lagerfeld's *A Line of Beauty* comes into and out of mode, but unlike fashion or  leaves of grass, Y will never come back to me. Instead, new images threaten to displace her in the RAM of the quotidian everyday. All I have are virtual images of her paintings that I cannot afford to buy. I see in those paintings her way of remembering the architecture of a home away from the home we have built here, in the city with stagnant air, as my student from Hong Kong calls it.

My regret doesn't change the fact that all her paintings have been sold out, or that I am not good enough to remember her without such aids.

Joe Hisashi's "Summer" plays and in the exhibit, I see a man bawling on the floor next to a flag representing the razor-sharp guillotine. I prefer the stubbiness of the succulent leaves like floating amoebas to memories of colored water I can no longer subdue. Watercolor once brought me so much joy, as the colors danced and transformed into flowers, dreams away from the city that never sleeps, dreams that take root in the image of a better world, of cherubs and the green fields in Central Park. But now, I brush water droplets off my urethane coat so that my cotton dress shirt will not be soaked with water. I want to rub away the dark pencil marks of memory, for the black sun to no longer shine so brightly as to burn me. As my nails dig into the skin below the water, I hope that maybe I'll stop myself before it stings.

**The Waiting Room – Daphne Rose** (she/her)

Several months before a procedure to remove a tumor from my mother's body, I learned that I had been admitted into the American University of Paris to study English literature. I was sixteen. I had spent the previous eleven months in a kind of cognitive waiting room anticipating, with dwindling patience, such a letter, but actually receiving it came as a surprise—I had forgotten I applied to AUP. With no 'dream college' to guide my choice, I had reached out to any school that struck me as interesting and didn't charge an application fee, including Reed College, the University of Tromsø, and the American University in Bulgaria. I had little intention of actually attending any of these schools but amused myself with the idea of them.

I'd expected to attend Mills College in Oakland, my mother's alma mater, but that previous summer, Mills had announced that it was shutting its doors. Whether or not it would reopen was unclear, and so I looked elsewhere. I was disappointed, mostly for my mother's sake—I didn't especially care where I went to college, as long as it was somewhere I could mention in a deceivingly indifferent voice at dinner parties, the sort of voice that people use when they want you to know how special they are but don't want to be perceived as braggarts. Yes, that's right, Bulgaria. Hand me the potatoes.

The tumor was found during a routine check-up. When the nurse called my mother in, I remained in the chilled, over-bright waiting room, pleather bench squeaking, as if in protest, when I crossed my legs. Her results were abnormal; we returned to the hospital for further testing. I chose a different bench further down the hallway, where I sat, occasionally glancing up from my anthology of feminist erotica, to watch strangers emerge from the pharmacy: old men with their sisters, or smartly-dressed lawyers talking loudly on the phone, or tired-looking women crawling

with children like feral cats with ticks.

My mother found me after her appointment. A small rod had been inserted into her body—a marker, used during ultrasounds to pinpoint the location of the tumor.

I remember it was a cool, sunlit spring afternoon, stinking of pollen, and so bright I had to squint, eyes streaming. We held hands as we left the hospital. My mother has elegant hands, with long, pale fingers and delicate wrists, hands I have always envied. In the car, I flipped through the materials the doctor had given her. The words BREAST CANCER were printed on each sheet of paper in enormous, bold black letters, as though whatever unfortunate individual was handed those papers needed the reminder. As though, despite the fact that the tumor needed to be biopsied before an official diagnosis was made, I would not repeat those words to myself, again and again, every hour of every day over the coming months.

Buttering toast: breast cancer.

Typing an email: breast cancer.

Brushing my teeth: bwust canshuh.

My monkey brain was incorrigible.

Being accepted to the American University of Paris fulfilled something in me. My extended family offered affection as a reward for achievement, rendering me dependent on academic validation for a sense of self-worth. In school, the path to success was clear—

enroll in Honors classes, study hard, read books with lots of big words that teachers *ooh* and *ahh* over—but after graduation, it became less so. At sixteen I was still very young. I had never been on a plane. To my recollection, I had never left Northern California.

I was deeply attached to my mother, who had raised me alone, and from whom I had never been apart for longer than the duration of a sleepover. Besides the emotional obstacles, there were the financial: my mother, a public school teacher, received no child support from my father. Even with help we could not afford the steep tuition of a glamorous private university in Europe. But, at home in California, the first two years of community college were free.

Though I knew I would save hundreds of thousands of dollars, I hated the idea of remaining in the quiet, lonely suburbs of my hometown, attending community college, while my friends and my ex-boyfriend scattered to colleges and universities up and down the West Coast: Reed, Lewis and Clark, UC Berkeley. I didn't feel pragmatic, I felt pathetic—but AUP blew them all out of the water. UC Berkeley might have been one of the greatest schools in the world, but I was the one leaving the United States. I was the one who would dip croissants in hot chocolate and attend classes with royalty and purchase vodka with my own ID before turning twenty-one. I fantasized about posting alluring black and white photos of myself on Instagram, wearing dark lipstick and smoking a cigarette and making bedroom eyes at the camera—never mind the fact that I didn't know how to smoke cigarettes and would never post such an image. I found a virtual tour of the AUP campus on the university's website, and I explored it from the safety of my bedroom, selecting the exact hideous orange-padded booth deep within the stacks of the library where I would sit and study for my classes, which would all have interesting names, like the Philosophy of Aesthetics and Introduction to Art Through Paris Museums.

I clung to the idea of Paris, of how *special* it would make me. Even as I enrolled at community college, I requested a deferral to the following year—by which time, I thought, perhaps I would be ready. A semester passed and I made no move towards Paris. Eventually I withdrew from AUP altogether. I would have done so even if my mother hadn't been ill—as difficult as it was to survive the proverbial waiting room of college acceptances, and how I dreaded facing it again, as desperately I yearned for external, academic validation, I loved my mother, and I wasn't prepared to leave her.

It's difficult to talk about cancer. We put our heads together and speak in hushed voices, as though afraid of being overheard, of attracting attention, like it's Bloody Mary in the mirror, and not the result of a single erroneous gene within one of 100 trillion cells. The average gambler has a one in 300 million chance of winning the lottery. Strange that, in the face of such considerable odds, cancer would be the world's second most common cause of death.

My mother returns to the hospital off Eureka to meet her surgeon—an attractive, black-haired woman in deep blue scrubs, with a soft, situationally-appropriate voice that has clearly been practiced in the mirror. I stand in the corner of the examination room, studying the ultrasound the surgeon put up, white light flashing before my uncomprehending eyes. My mother is sent to have her blood tested. Standing behind her chair, I hold our purses, wrinkling my nose at the cold stink of rubbing alcohol as the nurse disinfects the tender, bluish spot on the inside of her elbow. Mom averts her eyes, making conversation, but I watch the needle, watch her blood—such a deep shade of red, it appears black—slither through a thin plastic tube, into a vial. The room is so white, so sterile; her blood, so dark. I eavesdrop on her conversation with the nurse, a brown-skinned, dark-haired woman in middle age. A mother herself, she says. With all the finality of a woman zipping a body bag, the nurse corks and labels the vial of blood, lays it aside, and tapes a cotton pad over the pinprick in my mother's skin.

As a species, we are fascinated with blood—in particular, with its applications, and the connotations of its consumption. In cultures worldwide, bloodthirsty creatures—as ubiquitous as fried dumplings—slither into our collective consciousness: the strigoi and dhampirs of Slavic folklore; the Latin American chupacabras; the Madagascaran ramanga. Ancient Greeks poured blood over their altars as a gift to their gods. Ancient Egyptians bled their sick, and bloodletting remained a respectable medical practice until the 19th century. Through transubstantiation, Catholics drink the blood of Jesus at Mass as a reparation for their sin, and on Halloween nights, college girls dab their throats with sticky red paint and slurp vodka crans. Blood is salvation. Blood is power. Blood is release. I am relieved to live in a time where my mother's blood is drawn by nurses with sterile needles and not by drunk priestesses with veritable meat cleavers. How far we've come from ritual scarification. How far we have yet to go.

I didn't feel afraid, but I knew I was—how could I not be, when so abruptly faced with my mother's mortality? I don't think I feel fear the way most people do. As the child of an unhealthy family, I think I've been taught not to notice my fear, so that I am more easily manipulated. Instead, my distress makes itself known in other ways: for example, I become short-tempered and sensitive. I withdraw, unnerving my mother with my silence. I vomit, often. I develop night terrors. Once I reach a breaking point, I mention these symptoms to my mother, who wryly asks me if I'm under some stress. Only then does the lightbulb go off.

She must have been afraid, too, but it didn't show. She was as patient and loving and charismatic as ever. She continued to date, to mother me, to work, to read her books and drink her awful coffee.

The day of her surgery, I wake before her to give her the prescribed pseudo-Gatorade. The drink, I'm told, will wake up her body and kickstart the healing process. Our neighbor drives us to the hospital and we check in. The nurse gives me a visitor's badge and ushers me to a booth upstairs, in a long, shadowed hallway, where I sit for the next four hours reading Yeats and drinking burnt espresso, watching much more intelligent people rush past me in an endless current of blue-scrubbed competence. After five hours, I ache from sitting; I have been hit on twice by the same technician (I seem to be at my most alluring while sleep-deprived and hyperventilating); and I am in dire need of a restroom. I leave the building to take a walk. When I return, the nurses at the front desk look up at me, and then at the visitor's badge taped to my chest, and then back at their clipboards. Only once in my exploration am I stopped, and then, it's only by a kindly older man asking if I need directions. It occurs to me that, if I purchase a pack of visitor's badges at the office supply store, I can return whenever I want. I could be anyone. I could be some lunatic in search of coffee and an outlet to charge her laptop and a free Wi-Fi connection and quiet space to write, coming in just to get her work done. I make a note of it in case I ever have a deadline I urgently need to meet.

While wandering the surgical ward, both with the goal of stretching my legs and avoiding another run-in with the persistently flirtatious technician, I find the prayer room. It's dark, but I don't turn on the lights—I have a rule not to touch unfamiliar switches, lest I accidentally set off an alarm. I sit in silence for a few minutes. I peer out the window of the prayer room, into the atrium where I had said farewell to my mother hours prior. When I grow bored I pick up the Bible and flip through it. I smell it—dust and leather. I discover a bowl of paper slips, each with a name written on it in different handwriting. A flier stuck to the bulletin board informs me that a volunteer group will collect the slips next Sunday and read each patient's name aloud, praying for their health. I pick up the pencil, write out my mother's name, fold it, and drop it in the bowl, and then I leave the room.

My mother is released to me half an hour early. At home, I make mac and cheese for her, on request, and pretend not to breathe down her neck as she eats. There's nothing for her to do then but heal and wait.

Over the following weeks, I will come to feel as though I am standing in Yayoi Kusama's famous exhibit, "The Souls of Millions of Light Years Away"—a small, dimly-lit room in which every surface is reflective, creating an endless mirror that repeats visions of oneself on and on into oblivion; the ultimate liminal space, the threshold between the known and the unknown. As I await the results of my mother's biopsy I come to feel as if I exist in a constant liminal space, both physical—the waiting room of the surgical ward—and psychological: the place between high school and college, childhood and adulthood, between daughter and orphan, between worthy and worthless.

Liminal spaces are uncomfortable. The human mind isn't equipped to handle such a paradox, a place both transitional and ever-present, defined by a sense of comfort as well as unease. But the mind can adapt. With her exhibit, Kusama made liminal space a thing of exquisite and transformative beauty—not an in-between but a destination unto itself. After removing the bandage over the surgical site, my mother draws googly eyes over her healing incision, forming a smiley face, and gleefully shows it to me, delighted by her own artistic brilliance. Like Kusama and her mirrors, my mother is an expert at seeking the beauty in uncertainty, the virtue of the liminal, the blessings of the waiting room.

A month or so later, I stand in our kitchen making breakfast, smelling the hot coffee and fiery orange blossom incense. My mother comes in to show me the test results: the tumor is benign, and requires no further treatment. Holding her, I bury my face in her soft red hair and wonder who, in that hospital, in that poorly-lit room, read her name and prayed for her.

**winter in july – Jai-Michelle Louissen** (she/her)

the sleeping river in my body rouses. briny and swelling the upland bank. the rain, its own sea, fat and ample on my cheeks. light dissolves into water and clammy beckoning. the fish in the river whorl up in voices. songs from beyond the blue doorway.

midsummer fades into tempest. the sky here, slate and thickened with time wherein flakes of light wane their way to winter. i look at the water-cloyed air and the aftermath of storm felled trees and i remember the yin river, drifting. loss upwelling, forgotten in the rising luminance of spring. i stand draped in this, there is no escape. the hurricane's spiral, a mirror to my insensible sight.

and too, the orchids have fallen into the water and there is nothing i can do to stop it. they have sunken into my dreams and spilt their pollen. i, like miranda on the tide, return, circumfluous and proliferating in the squall broken remnants of trees and roses thrashed into memory.

winter flooded the garden in the first two days of july.

**On the Fourth of July – S. Kavi** (she/her)


       No Indian food today. Only American. All American. Dad wakes up early in the morning to start smoking the brisket before the Texas heat swells into the day. He fires up the grill, ready with Fourth of July food staples. Hot dogs. Beef patties. Chicken drumsticks smothered in barbeque sauce. Corn on the cob. Mom wakes up early, but lets her children sleep in as she heads to the kitchen. She ties an apron around her, knowing that she will need it upon looking at the ingredients in front of her. Granny smith apples. Cold butter. Brown sugar. Flour. Eggs. Her children rub their eyes as they come from their rooms about three hours later, following the scent of the fresh-baked apple pie. Mom tells the story of how it was the first American food she learned to make once coming from Kerala. How her first pie was sour from not enough sugar and the wrong kind of apples. How she overcooked many pies in her day. How many times she burned pies and set the house on fire. Her children hold back their giggles, but much like any good mother, she can see through them easily. Mom lightly slaps the poking fingers heading to her homemade pie and tells her children to get dressed. She has a fun game for them to play.

Mom takes the kids to the store with her. She turns the shopping list into a scavenger hunt. If they can find all the items she asks for, they get popsicles. Kids go sprinting down every aisle grabbing items off the shelves. Red solo cups. Napkins. Paper plates with the orange flowers on them. White sugar. Potato salad. Peaches. Milk chocolate bars. Graham crackers. Marshmallows. The large yellow bottle of lemon juice. Crinkle-cut BBQ potato chips in a red bag. They win her game. Mom opens the large freezer door to the popsicles as her children make their selection: the red, white, and blue striped ones that are shaped like a rocket. She tells them to wait until lunch to enjoy them to avoid spoiling their appetite.

       Mom finds the large pitcher and starts making lemonade. White sugar makes the sour mingle of lemon juice and water all the more sweeter. She adds her not-so secret ingredient of peach juice along with slices of the fruit into the pitcher. The last thing she adds is the ice, making the pitcher frosty with cool dew settling on the surface of the glass. The other aunties who arrived so far ask if they can help her in any way. She smiles while wiping the sweat off her brow to tell them she has it all under control. Once she brings the pitcher to the backyard, she summons everyone to gather.

We gather around noon in the backyard. The rich smell of smoked brisket calls to all of us. We say a prayer before grabbing our plates. Thank the Lord for giving us a life in this country. For bringing us together to celebrate what freedoms we possess. Once we say, "Amen," we dig into the barbequed feast. Aunties wearing sunglasses and striped capri pants while sipping lemonade with their feet in the water. The teenagers take a break from their phones to make s'mores around the campfire. Little kids running around the trees in the backyard with red, white, and blue popsicles melting down their brown skin. As evening reaches, everyone in town comes together to watch the fireworks in the neighborhood park. Families from every neighborhood and every background. A vendor passes out sparklers to the crowd and glowsticks to the kids. Another vendor hands out sno-cones to everyone. Children stick out their colorful tongues at each other, unable to contain their giggles. Dads hold their children on their shoulders so they can see the show. All of them smile at the sight of exploding colors in the night sky. All of them, no matter the color of their skin or the sound of their voice.

We are all American during this day. The one day we have no doubt that we belong in this country. We take it in, the feeling of freedom, as we live in our temporary American Dream.

# ABOUT THE CONTRIBUTORS

❖ A. Bhardwaj (she/her) writes and reads whenever she can. She loves drawing inspiration from the world around her and her daily experiences. She enjoys writing poems and short stories but has been exploring songwriting recently.

❖ April Renee (she/her) is a poet residing in Portland, Oregon. April has been writing and performing poetry since age nine and views writing as an opportunity to explore her identity as a queer disabled woman. April's work has appeared in Eunoia Review, Feral Journal of Poetry and Art, Pile Press, and others.

❖ c. michael kinsella writes because he has to.

❖ Cara could tell you many things about herself, most of which are true but few that would make sense. Her work is often uncomfortably, brutally honest and interrogates trauma in a way which might not be completely healthy. The poetry is melancholy and angry but tells the story of evolving identity and the ever-present spectrum of mental health. You can find her and her sadness @polar_truths on Instagram.

❖ Chris Sadhill is a fringe writer of the dark, exploring common themes of death, poverty, society, and love. Sadhill's career started in 2017 having co-wrote various films under his birth name. He is passionate about creating thought-provoking content that examines the human soul and challenges our conversations. He resides near State College, PA with his wife and two evil cats.

❖ Claire Thom, originally from Scotland, is EIC and founder of The Wee Sparrow Poetry Press. She has had poems published by a variety of presses and she was long-listed for the Erbacce Poetry Prize in 2021, 2022, and 2023. She is also a Touchstone Haiku Award.

❖ Dan Flore III's poems have appeared in many publications. His 6 poetry books are Lapping Water, Humbled Wise Men Christmas Haikus, Home and other places I've yet to see, Pink Marigold Rays,(Gen Z Publishing) Written in the dust on the ceiling fan, (Dead Man's Press Ink.) and Hospital Issued Writing Notebook.(Querencia Press)

❖ Daniel Moreschi is a poet from Neath, South Wales, UK. After life was turned upside down by his ongoing battle with severe M.E., he rediscovered his passion for poetry that had been dormant since his teenage years. Writing has served as a distraction from his struggles ever since. Daniel has been acclaimed by many poetry competitions, including the annual ones hosted by the Oliver Goldsmith Literature Festival, Wine Country Writers Festival, Short Stories Unlimited, Michigan Poetry Society, Ohio Poetry Day, Anansi Archive, Westmoreland Arts &

Heritage Festival, and Inchicore Ledwidge Society. Daniel has also had poetry published by The Society of Classical Poets.

❖ Daphne Rose is an author, poet, and editor. She studied fiction at the Writing Institute at Sarah Lawrence College and at the University of Iowa, and she is the editor-in-chief and founder of Sequoia Speaks, a print-based literary journal. Her work is published or forthcoming in The Fourth River, BarBar, and Assignment Magazine.

❖ Debra K. Every is the author of many short stories and, to date, two completed novels. Her novel, DEENA UNDONE is one of four finalists in the *When Words Count Book Deal* competition. Her short stories have appeared in *Unleash Creatives* and *Arzono Publishing's 2023 Anthology*.

❖ Deirdre Garr Johns (she/her) resides in South Carolina with her family. Nature is an inspiration, and poetry is a first love. Much of her work is inspired by memories of people and places. Her poetry has appeared in *Sylvia Magazine, South Carolina Bards Poetry Anthology, Eunoia Magazine, Nymeria Magazine, Sasee Magazine, Silver Birch Press*, and more. Her website is www.amuseofonesown.com.

❖ Dia VanGunten did not eat pink horseshoes on her 8th birthday. She does write magical realism. "En Caul" is part of a larger project that explores the stories we tell, the stories we don't tell and how we mythologize to survive.

❖ Eo Sivia (She/Her) likes to write about it. All the things, all the time. She's probably writing about it as we speak. She also enjoys being in the garden and soaking up the joy that comes from flowers and nature. Her Instagram account (esb.poems) is filled with photos and videos that she has taken, mostly of the wonderful things you can only find outside.

❖ Eric Burgoyne writes from his home on the North Shore of Oahu, Hawaii. He has a Master of Arts in Creative Writing and MBA focused on Communications. His poems have appeared in Lothlorien Poetry Journal, The Dawntreader, Paddler Press, and elsewhere.

❖ Exodus Oktavia Brownlow, she/her, is a writer, budding beekeeper, and a rising seamstress currently residing in the enchanting pine tree forest of Blackhawk, Ms. She is a graduate of Mississippi Valley State University with a BA in English, and Mississippi University for Women with an MFA in Creative Writing. Exodus has been published or has forthcoming work with *Electric Lit, West Branch, Denver Quarterly, F(r)iction* and more. Her writing has been selected for Best MicroFiction [2022 and 2021], and Wigleaf Top 50 [2022]. She is the recipient of the 2022 "The Changing American South" fellowship at the Writers' Colony at Dairy Hollow, and serves as an Associate Editor with Fractured Lit. Exodus has perfected the French Seam by hand, and is unequivocally in love with the color green. You can find her at exodusoktaviabrownlow.com.

❖ George Oliver has just finished a PhD on contemporary fiction at King's College London, where he also taught American literature for three years. He is both a short fiction and culture writer, and Assistant Editor at *Coastal Shelf*. His short stories have recently appeared in *Avatar Review*, *BRUISER*, *Clackamas Literary Review*, and *Watershed Review*, and he was shortlisted for Ouen Press' 2019 Short Story Competition.

❖ Giada Nizzoli (she/her) is an Italian, UK-based freelance writer and copywriter. She's the author of the poetry collection *Will-o'-the-Wisps*, the magical realism short story collection *Set in Marble*, and the poetry pamphlet *Ghost Hometowns*. Her work also appeared in *The London Magazine*, *October Hill Magazine*, *Ink Sac* by Cephalopress, the anthology *Depression is what really killed the dinosaurs* by Sunday Mornings at the River, and *The Pangolin Review*. She shares her work and writing journey with her social media communities, and you can find out more about her at giadanizzoli.co.uk.

❖ Jai-Michelle is a Scottish poet, living by the dune swept edges of The Netherlands. Published in various journals, her first chapbook published in 2022 by Sunday Mornings at the River. She is also an editor of a small literary publication the winged moon magazine.

❖ Jasmine Luck (she/her) writes romance, science fiction, and poetry. Her short fiction has appeared in three anthologies to date and her novel *Sugar Rush* was released earlier this year. Her dual heritage (Chinese-Malay and British) is a constant source of inspiration.

❖ J.D. Gevry (they/them; fae/faer; he/him) is an emerging poet from Vermont whose work is shaped by their experiences as a queer, polyamorous, non-binary trans person with a disability. Their work has appeared or is forthcoming in "The Bitchin' Kitsch," "just femme and dandy," "Remington Review," and "Lit Shark," among others. J.D. is currently writing a book of poetry chronicling the accidental development of a queer romantic affair. Fae is passionate about community wellbeing and holds a bachelor's degree in human sexuality and Master of Public Health concentrated on LGBTQ+ sexual health and wellness.

❖ Jen Schneider is a community college educator who lives, works, and writes in small spaces throughout Pennsylvania.

❖ K. Jasmin Dulai lives in the Bay Area of California where she works with social justice and arts nonprofits. Her work has appeared in The Citron Review, Feral: A Journal of Poetry and Art, Glass: A Journal of Poetry, Pretty Owl Poetry, So to Speak, The Eastern Iowa Review, Drunk Monkeys, trampset, and other publications. She is a 2022 VONA/Voices (Voices of Our Nation Arts Foundation) alum in poetry, a 2023 VONA alum in experimental writing, and participated in the Kenyon Review Writers Workshop for poetry in 2021. She can be found on Twitter as @kjdulai.

❖ Kara's short stories, poetry and essays have appeared in Hobart After Dark, Door is A Jar, Marrow, Birthing Magazine, and elsewhere. She lives with her family in an antique farmhouse in rural New Hampshire. You can connect with her on Instagram and Twitter @karaqwrites or by visiting her website, www.karaqwrites.com

- ❖ Kelly Dillahunt (she/her) is a queer former librarian who grew up in a trailer park outside Dayton, Ohio. Now, she fixes houses and writes things. Kelly's work has previously been featured in *Anti-Heroin Chic*.

- ❖ Kit E. Lascher is an art corvid. She collects anything shiny, holds her collaborators close, and always remembers. You can find her work in magazines and anthologies, including beestung (Nominated for Best American Science Fiction/Fantasy 2023), The Winnow, Hearth & Coffin, and Mid-Level Management Literary Magazine. She is an editorial team member at Punk Monk Magazine and the editor of Trash Wonderland. She can be found at trashwonderland.com.

- ❖ KRISTINE ESSER SLENTZ is the author of *woman, depose* (FlowerSong Press 2021). She is originally from northwest Indiana and the Chicagoland area. She earned her MFA in Creative Writing (poetry) in May 2020 from City College of New York (CCNY) where she is currently an Adjunct Assistant Professor. KRISTINE is a Pushcart Prize nominee, finalist in the Glass Poetry Chapbook and F(r)iction's Flash Fiction Contests, recipient of a CCNY English Department Teacher-Writer Award, and former Rifkind Fellow and Poets Afloat resident. Currently, she is the co-founder and organizer/host of the monthly artist series, Adverse Abstraction, in NYC's East Village.

- ❖ Kushal Poddar, the author of 'Postmarked Quarantine' has eight books to his credit. He is a journalist, father, and the editor of 'Words Surfacing'. His works have been translated into twelve languages, published across the globe. Twitter- https://twitter.com/Kushalpoe

- ❖ Leonie Anderson developed a passion for writing as a young girl on the island of Jamaica. Growing up beside her neighborhood library, Leonie would spend endless hours exploring the fascinating world that authors created through their compelling fictional works. This awakened her love for reading and writing. Her favorite genres are mystery and fantasy, but she prefers to write emotional poetry and realistic fiction. She migrated from the Caribbean, and now resides in the United States, where she teaches English Language Arts, and spend her days secretly trying to instill a of love of language and reading in her kids. Leonie is a published poet, relationship blogger, and nature enthusiast. She believes that poetry is able to "describe the indescribable, love the unlovable, feel the undeniable, and grieves with the inconsolable". She contends that this aforementioned quote is the principal reason she is impelled to write.

- ❖ Lesley Rogers Hobbs (she/her) is an Irish poet and artist living in the Pacific Northwest (US) with her husband and service dog. She loves popcorn, sunshine, Pink Floyd and the ocean. Her poetry has been published by *The Ekphrastic Review, Open Door Poetry* and upcoming in *The Hyacinth Review*.

- ❖ Linda M. Crate (she/her) is a Pennsylvanian writer whose poetry, short stories, articles, and reviews have been published in a myriad of magazines both online and in print. She has twelve published chapbooks the latest being: Searching Stained Glass Windows For An Answer (Alien Buddha Publishing, December 2022). She is also the author of the novella Mates (Alien Buddha Publishing, March 2022). Her debut book of photography *Songs of the Creek* (Alien Buddha Publishing, April 2023) was recently published.

- ❖ Native New Yorker LindaAnn LoSchiavo, a four time nominee for The Pushcart Prize, has also been nominated for Best of the Net, the Rhysling Award, and Dwarf Stars. Elgin Award winner "A Route Obscure and Lonely," "Women Who Were Warned," Firecracker Award and IPPY Award nominee "Messengers of the Macabre" [co-written with David Davies], "Apprenticed to the Night" [UniVerse Press, 2023], and "Felones de Se: Poems about Suicide" [Ukiyoto Publishing, 2023] are her latest poetry titles. In 2023, her poetry placed as a finalist in Thirty West Publishing's "Fresh Start Contest" and in the 8th annual Stephen DiBiase contest.

- ❖ Liz Bajjalieh (She/they/he) is a Chicago-based queer and nonbinary writer whose work focuses on the raw world of healing, the soft world of spiritual journeys, and the curious world of community building. He is currently published in Friend's Journal and Diminuendo, and is in process of publishing her first poetry collection with Fernwood Press. Liz is also a mixed media 2D artist who hosts local community vision board events. Their additional works can be found on @dandelion.tea.art.

- ❖ Meghan King is a Jersey born and raised writer. Meghan's most recent work is in Not Ghosts, But Spirits Vol I, Winter Anthology 2023, and forth coming Not Ghosts, But Spirits Vol III from Querencia Press. She was first published in NJ Bards Poetry Review 2022 by Local Gems Press. She writes poetry and nonfiction on the resilience of the human spirit. Meghan finds confidence honing her craft attending writing workshops and open mic nights held by Arts by the People. She holds to the belief in being able to change the tide.

- ❖ Mousai Kalliope (she/her) is a Brazilian born, Portugal raised, English writing poetess who has been writing since she was 12. Her upcoming book A constellation of dreams is a collection of intrusive thoughts. She is 22 years old and a scorpio.

- ❖ Nathalia is a hobby writer who lives in the Middle East. A journalist by profession with a career that spans over a decade, she has had articles published in newspapers and magazines in India and the Middle East. Nathalia started exploring creative writing by posting her work on Instagram and Twitter. Social media handles IG; @nat_writerslife Twitter: @saltedcaramelle

- ❖ Nick Ferryman grew up in the shadow of Savannah, Georgia, where the shade of live oaks and the shades of the formerly living are no strangers. Vivid settings, haunted by nostalgia, mark his tales of love, loss, lust, and vengeance. He can be reached at ferrymansilver@gmail.com.

- ❖ Pelle Zingel is an author and artist from Sønderborg in Denmark. Born 2 June 1998. Pelle is a self-taught artist, when Pelle is writing and performing, he uses his bad and good life experiences, he also uses his skills as an actor to create different emotions. Through his artistic skills he wants to be a sound and a lighthouse, which shines and echoing around the world. Pelle has performed his poetry in Denmark, Germany & online in New York. Pelle published his poetry collection " Mental Harddisk X-rays" 2022. Pelle has his poetry published in 3 anthologies and 3 magazines in Denmark, 6 anthologies in USA, 1 magazine in England.

- Rachael Collins (she/her) has never had her work published, other than the inclusion of an exceptionally over dramatic poem entitled "The Fox" in a grade school writing anthology. Nevertheless, observing the world around her and attempting to share it, as well as her own experiences, through words has remained a lifelong constant. She often writes about feeling anything but heroic while working as a nurse, longing for faith, her mental health journey, and memories involving shopping malls. She lives in Seattle with her partner and two "lucky" black cats, despite a lifelong fear of felines.

- S. Kavi is a South Indian American poet, writer, and artist from Texas. Her work explores her cultural experiences, nostalgia, and healing. She was a finalist for Best of the Net 2023 and her work appears in antonym, Culinary Origami, Metachrosis, and elsewhere.

- Sadee Bee is a queer artist and writer inspired by magic, strange dreams, and creepy vibes. Sadee is the Visual Arts Editor for Sage Cigarettes Magazine and the author of Pupa: Growth & Metamorphosis and Magic Lives In Girls. Sadee can be found on the web at linktr.ee/SadeeBee.

- Saira Khan's writing has appeared (or is forthcoming) in *Pleiades*, *Hennepin Review*, *Olney Magazine*, *Identity Theory* and elsewhere. Her short fiction chapbook, *Late Stage* is available from DeRailleur Press in Brooklyn NY. She is a recipient of an Open Door Career Advancement Grant from Poets & Writers Magazine, funded by Reese Witherspoon. She has workshopped at Hedgebrook, One Story Summer Conference, Tin House Summer Conference and Writers in Paradise at Eckerd College. Her work was shortlisted for the 2023 Coppice Prize in short fiction. She is a 2023 Periplus Fellow.

- Sara Sabharwal is a poetess and author from central Illinois. Her ambition is to bring beauty and whimsy to every situation. She can be found on instagram @sarasabharwal.poetry

- Sophie Dickinson (she/they) is a poet and writer from Chicago, Illinois. She has had work published in Labyrinth Anthologies, Beyond the Veil Press, Seaglass Literary, Querencia Press, and Erato Magazine. They use poetry and writing as a therapeutic tool for themself and a way to learn the stories of those around them. Her own work attempts to bridge the emotional to the visceral and explore the ways our emotional and mental lives are embodied in the physical world.

- Stephanie Parent is an author of dark fiction and poetry. Her debut horror novel *The Briars* was published by Cemetery Gates Media, and her debut poetry collection *Every Poem a Potion, Every Song a Spell* was published by Querencia Press.

- Tiffany Troy is a critic, translator, and poet. She is the author of *Dominus* (BlazeVOX) and the chapbook *When Ilium Burns* (Bottlecap Press), as well as co-translator of Santiago Acosta's *The Coming Desert / El próximo desierto* (Alliteration Publishing House), in collaboration with Acosta and the Women in Translation project at the University of Wisconsin. Her reviews and interviews are published in *The Adroit Journal, The Cortland Review, The Los Angeles Review, The Laurel Review, EcoTheo Review, Rain Taxi, New World Writing,* the *Hong Kong Review of Books, and Tupelo Quarterly,* where she is Managing Editor.

- Tom Squitieri is a three-time winner of the Overseas Press Club and White House Correspondents' Association awards for work as a war correspondent. He is blessed to have his poetry appear in several publications, books and anthologies, the art exhibition Color: Story2020/2021, and the film "Fate's Shadow: The Whole Story," where he shared the Los Angeles Motion Picture Festival "Grand Jury Prize Gold for Monologues & Poetry." He writes most of his poetry while parallel parking or walking his dogs, Topsie and Batman.

- tommy wyatt (he/they) is the author of *NOW THAT'S WHAT I CALL HORROR!* (Gutslut Press), *So, Who's Courage?* (Bullshit Lit), *JETTISONED* (selfpub), TASEREDGED (WATCH OUT!) (Querencia Press), and others. he's currently writing about dissociation and the things that go bump in the night, and probably is reading *Goodnight Punpun* as his cat, Cosmo, is by his side.

- Uchechukwu Onyedikam is a Nigerian creative artist based in Lagos, Nigeria. His poems have appeared in *Amsterdam Quarterly, Brittle Paper, Poetic Africa, Hood Communists* and in print anthologies. Christina Chin and he have co-published *Pouring Light on the Hills* (2022).

- Willow Page Delp (they/them) is a writer, reader, and book reviewer.

- wren pflock (they/them) is a young queer writer from australia. they have been published in a local magazine and want nothing more than to expand their portfolio. they write about grappling with identity and life with mental illness. wren was the top english student in their class and chooses to not use capital letters out of spite.

- Xiomarra Milann is a Chicana writer based in Laredo, TX who is trying really hard to make the person who said "those who can't do, teach" turn in their grave. In her free time, she is the host of the "ButUmmYeah" podcast and painter of fruits on ceramic coasters. She was a finalist in the 2023 Battle on the Border Poetry Slam and hopes in her next life she'll be born as something with wings. You can find her @xiomilann on Instagram and read her work in DVINO Magazine, Sam Fiftyfour Literary, Medium, Infrarrealista Review, Ink & Marrow Lit and on her 6th grade creative writing teacher's bulletin board. Her work is forthcoming in The Sybil Journal and Acentos Review.

# OTHER TITLES FROM QUERENCIA

*Allison by Marisa Silva-Dunbar*

*GIRL. by Robin Williams*

*Retail Park by Samuel Millar*

*Every Poem a Potion, Every Song a Spell by Stephanie Parent*

*songs of the blood by Kate MacAlister*

*Love Me Louder by Tyler Hurula*

*God is a Woman by TJ McGowan*

*Learning to Float by Alyson Tait*

*Fever by Shilo Niziolek*

*Cutting Apples by Jomé Rain*

*Girl Bred from the 90s by Olivia Delgado*

*Wax by Padraig Hogan*

*When Memory Fades by Faye Alexandra Rose*

*The Wild Parrots of Marigny by Diane Elayne Dees*

*Hospital Issued Writing Notebook by Dan Flore III*

*Knees in the Garden by Christina D Rodriguez*

*Provocative is a Girl's Name by Mimi Flood*

*Bad Omens by Jessica Drake-Thomas*

*Beneath the Light by Laura Lewis-Waters*

*Ghost Hometowns by Giada Nizzoli*

*Dreamsoak by Will Russo*

*the abyss is staring back by nat raum*

*How Long Your Roots Have Grown by Sophia-Maria Nicolopoulos*

*The World Eats Butterflies Like You by Isabelle Quilty*

*Playing Time in tongues by Vita Lerman*

*unloving the knife by Lilith Kerr*

*5 Spirits in My Mouth by Pan Morigan*

*You Shouldn't Worry About the Frogs by Eliza Marley*

*Now Let's Get Brunch: A Collection of RuPaul's Drag Race Twitter Poetry by Alex Carrigan*

*The Dissection of a Tiger by Tyler Walter*

*Reasons Why We're Angry by Sophia Isabella Murray*

*An Absurd Palate by Alysa Levi-D'Ancona*

*Tender is the Body by Alise Versella*

*Stained: an anthology of writing about menstruation*

*The Beginning of Leaving by Elsa Valmidiano*

*House of Filth by Kei Vough Korede*

*TASEREDGED (watch out!) by Tommy Wyatt*

*Dear Nora, by c. michael kinsella*

Printed in the USA
CPSIA information can be obtained
at www.ICGtesting.com
LVHW051115310723
753624LV00018B/866